The Absolution Game

THE
ABSOLUTION
GAME

Paul Sayer

Constable · London

First published in Great Britain 1992
by Constable and Company Limited
3 The Lanchesters, 162 Fulham Palace Road
London W6 9ER
© 1992 Paul Sayer
The right of Paul Sayer to be identified
as the author of this work
has been asserted by him in accordance
with the Copyright, Designs and Patents Act 1988
ISBN 0 09 471460 6
Set in Linotron 11pt Palatino by
Falcon Typographic Art Ltd, Fife, Scotland
Printed in Great Britain by
St Edmundsbury Press Limited
Bury St Edmunds, Suffolk

A CIP catalogue record for this book
is available from the British Library

To my father, Jack Sayer

PART 1

Let me first say that I did not embark on this life with the intention of killing anyone. It's a feeble refutation, I know. But true. True enough. Indeed, haven't I always believed in the sacredness of human existence, in whatever breathy form, high or low, it might take? Rare that, these days, some would say. And I might agree now that things have reached this sorry pass. Once though, I really did see myself as saintly, a good man. A martyr? Perhaps.

So, what went wrong?

I can't say for sure. There was a rumbling in the blood. A sea change. And . . . it happened.

Oh, I have killed. Taken a life. Call it what you will, I am a murderer. And by the time you read this I shall either be in the goodly state custody I deserve or I will have taken the lesser option of doing away with myself, to clutter and muddle the world no more with my heavy presence. I should get on. My revelations here will help me make up my mind which way I should jump and I am anxious to see how I shall perform, how it all might end.

First, a little history, the recounting of that troublesome business of my piety.

I was never so good. Not all my life. Certainly not towards the end. But in the beginning, well . . . I'll recall myself at the age of seven or eight bringing the morning paper for our next-door neighbour. I never knew what was wrong with him. Something to do with his nerves, I thought. But I knew he was dying and that I was to be nice to him, to be good. I'd take the paper up to his bedroom where he lay, bones rattling, extending a feeble yellow hand, slavering his thanks. My mother would kiss me for the deed. Daily. And I was made good, sanctified, pure. I'll remember too befriending the bullied class weakling, coolly lecturing his amused tormentors about the evil of their ways. They'd slope off, confused, sniggering, while I turned to my admiring friend, quietly triumphant. And I recollect – can you believe it? – helping the old people across the busy road that ran through the middle of our village. The opportunities to display my wilful kindness were many and I could not resist a single one. My father began to fret. And once I heard him say to my mother, 'Daft in a boy, all that caring. Needs to look out for number one, he does. Nobody else will.' But she simply remarked that it was lovely to see and that it would only be a passing phase.

But it wasn't. It stayed with me, troubled me on into my adult life when I gave up my job as an engineer to become, of course, a social worker.

I had married by then, though Caroline, my wife, originally suspected little of my altruistic tendencies. At first she said she understood, yet she was put out when, after I had qualified, I said I wanted to start a new life, to move north where I felt my talents would be of greatest use. I encouraged and coerced, remonstrated with her about the emptiness of our cosy rural life. She was no match for me, I realize it now, had no argument she could pit against the power and certain belief I had in my philanthropy, my goodness. In the end she gave in and came with me. And I'll picture now, while I can, our arrival in this town, our standing outside the station watching the skyline of purple-slated houses, the floodlights of the rugby league ground, the smoke rising from the liquorice factory chimney and, beneath the advertising hoardings opposite, a group of white-faced, angular women, clutching the straps of their patent leather handbags, ducking every now and then to peer into the windscreens of cruising cars.

'Oh dear,' said Caroline.

'They're all right,' I said. 'They need help. That's all.'

To impress my wife, I went over to them, asked how I could help get them out of this mess, told them I was a social worker.

'Gerrout of it,' said one, looking to the street, holding herself against the cold, relaxing her stance every time a possible customer drove past.

'Go on,' offered another. 'We're all right. Don't need the likes of you, interfering, spoilin' things. Away. Fuck off,' she said angrily as a car pulled from the curb without her, its driver troubled by my presence.

I laughed and left them to it. Clearly, I had much to learn (and a thick skin to develop – I was never again so naïve, so trusting in dealing with my clients). But I was exhilarated – my ministrations among the deprived, the deranged, the homeless, the abused and the abusing, had begun for real.

Over those first few months Caroline did her best to understand, finding work of her own, teaching in an infants' school on the east side of the river. She even came with me to the pubs where I insisted we visit to see the town at its most revealing, the factory lads slaking their powerful thirsts, the girls in satellite groups, cackling in their wake. And we found a snug little house with two bedrooms, a bathroom upstairs, a single skeletal rose bush with rusted foliage in the tiny forecourt garden. It was one of the better terraced houses in the town, certainly the best we could afford on my reduced salary, though it was only one third the size of the place we'd left down south.

'It's not a bad spot,' I said. 'I'm near my work here. Once people get to know us . . .'

But she was not happy. I knew it. And one day I came home to find her in tears. Her car had been ransacked by the kids, the seats ripped, a dead rat left hanging from the rearview mirror, some vile scrawl made on the windscreen with her own lipstick.

'The little sods,' I said, trying to make light of the situation.

'That's all you've got to say, is it?' She was shivering

with anger, lipstick smears on her hands and her swishy white dress.

'Come on, Caroline. They're just kids.'

'Do something about it. Get the police.'

'What good will that do?'

'It'll do me good. They're bad children . . . people,' she said between sobs. 'They come from rotten bad homes and they'll make evil rotten adults. Why can't you see that? Why do you have to go on . . . oh, forgiving them all the bloody time?'

'Someone has to.'

'But why you? Why me? I hate it here, Robert. I bloody, bloody hate it.'

She composed herself then, an ugly distant calm informing her expression.

'It's them or me. Choose. Let me know when you've made up your mind.'

It's a fact that I was just trying to make a point with her, pursuing it madly, seeing in her a token of whatever it was that I disliked about humankind, that needed to be put to rights.

Madness. All of it.

Sixteen years have passed since that day. (And was it at the very moment of Caroline's departure that I noticed a tightening of the waistband of my trousers, the flesh running soft and loose on my arms and buttocks? I ate no more than usual, worked even harder to put aside the dull pain of her leaving me, an ache that I wanted to deny existed. But within three weeks, if my memory is not playing tricks on me, I became fat – rolls of skin above the knees, lumps and blobs everywhere, even my toes seemed bigger. A curious, queer business, that.)

After Caroline left I narrowed my life, gave it sharply defined limits. I had my work, the house where I have remained to this day, a life of sorts. I would offer my affections for the human race through my work, its cool officialdom, by proxy. I needed no one close, I thought, believing I could live without that particular complication, the appalling intimacy of love, marriage.

And the years went by, I grew older, suffering the affections of no one, save for two brief and calamitous dalliances which served only to reinforce my wish for aloofness. But it was a long time to be caring, mindful only of the needs of others. And I was never so pure as I'd set out to be. If only I had been a little more selfish, more true to my natural urges. I remember these and other doubts arriving one morning last year, on the day of my forty-third birthday. They came in a tumbling heap, already half-known, information I had ruggedly kept from myself. I had no one to celebrate that day with – I felt lonely probably for the first time in my life. And I felt the first glimmerings of a need, not for the maturity I foolishly believed came with age, rather for its opposite, for life to control me, for me to become its subject, yes, its victim. Without really noticing it I had already been making odd gestures like allowing myself a television set after ten years' abstinence from the things, hanging around the pubs – the heart and lungs of a place like this – and taking long solitary walks (when once I found myself staring and staring at a funeral party, my head and bowels full of the most unsettling mixture of satisfaction and fear . . .). There was, it seemed, someone else inside me. Can you imagine the horror of such a discovery, of an invading party in your own mind, the one place from which you cannot flee? Try not to think about it. It will do you no good.

But this is getting us nowhere, the raking up of my past, this mucking about. I'm making things too plain, offering too many clues with my pointless history. Now I must insist on you, the recipient of this unstoppable document – be it a suicide note or the catalogue of evidence I shall offer for use against me – doing some of the work yourself. I shall try to be restrained, unsentimental, though there must be some dissimulation, I think, for both our sakes. Oh, let's be on with it. You want facts? The truth, perhaps? On then. The cast is assembling, the frail, the disposable, the only woman I think I ever truly loved, and one strange waif of a boy whose fate became inexorably tangled with my own. And more. The demons I have unleashed are beginning their march apace, jostling for attention. So . . .

It's a Thursday, some months ago, and I'm sitting at my desk in the health centre office I share with Malcolm, a social worker colleague. Outside the clouds are grey and swollen and low (Does that matter? To me. Each moment, each detail . . .). But inside we are both scribbling our notes with a tacit sense of relief, suffering the luxury of reprieve now that our working day is almost over. Occasionally one of us breaks the silence to exchange some fragment, some cameo of an event that has befallen us in the last nine hours. For myself I recount a visit that afternoon with old Maisie Bertowski, one of my many clients. She is like thousands in this town, trying to eke out the last of her days in her own home, a rundown cottage on the west side of town. Her grip on life, on her memory and identity, is becoming more suspect with each passing day. She was in a rare state when I found her, I tell Malcolm. Can he believe that I found a plate of her own faeces in the oven? Malcolm throws his head back, beating the desk with his fists, guffawing loud enough to be heard throughout the building.

'We sh-shouldn't laugh, Robert. N-not really.'

'But we have to, Malcolm. We must.'

And it's true. True enough. Part, perhaps, of the way I'm thinking these days.

Malcolm peghs, sniffs and for a few seconds he's staring at me, wall-eyed like a rabbit in a trap, the pale manic smile still fixed in the wires of his beard long after the moment of humour has passed.

[15]

'Did her a few spuds to go with it,' I say. 'Apple crumble for afters.'

But this does not register with him at all and, with a troubled huff, he bends over his work once more.

Poor Malcolm. It's three months before this when he's barging through the check-out of a supermarket with his gloomy, hunted look, stammer clenched between his teeth. In his arms are a Barbie doll, a bottle of scotch, and a huge shank of ham. Malcolm, childless, teetotal, vegetarian, has no need of these things, nor has he any intention of either trying to conceal or paying for them. It's a hopeless business, the scuffle with the manager outside the poster-decked windows, the night in the cells without his belt and tie and shoelaces. In court they put it down to the pressure of work, something which we in the profession sadly understand all too well. In view of his previously untarnished record and what the magistrate refers to as Malcolm's value to society, he's let off with a conditional discharge, though I wonder sometimes if it might not have been a greater kindness to prosecute, to tell Malcolm that he need trouble himself no more with the problems of others. Rycott, the director of social services, asked me to keep an eye on him, though I cannot vouch for Malcolm's future – he's a hollow man now. No more caring in him.

In the silence that follows, I write in my own notes that I cleaned up Maisie's place, made sure she had a proper meal in front of her, then rang her GP. And I am, in fact, waiting for him to get back to me, to agree the obvious – that we must get the old lady in some place, anywhere we can scrounge a bed – when the phone does indeed ring. But it's not the doctor's voice I hear. This is Sergeant Mackie. He tells me they've had a complaint about some kid pissing in the street. His name's William Duff and he's living with a few old winos in a derelict house on the Brocken estate. 'Deal with him,' he says. 'Or it's down to us.'

I replace the receiver, sighing softly to myself, ignoring a sideways glance from Malcolm.

'T-trouble?'

[16]

'Nothing serious.'

'Anything I c-could help with?'

'No. Thanks, Malcolm. It's nothing.'

'I'd be only t-too happy to h-help if I can, Robert.'

'That's nice. But really, I can manage.'

'G-good,' Malcolm says with a spluttered grin, swiping non-existent bits of fluff from the sleeve of his jacket. 'Th-that's really good.'

I look at him again. So young. Can't be more than thirty. Divorced last year. Sad Malcolm. Poor Malcolm. The phrases trip through my mind again. To help him feel useful I ask him if he wouldn't mind taking a message from Maisie's GP, should he ring. Then I lift my mac from the drawer of a filing cabinet and make my way out through an adjoining doctor's waiting room and its cherry-faced occupants washed up by the cold dusk.

Over the years I have developed a tardiness when responding to calls such as this. If I hang around long enough a problem may well resolve itself before I arrive, adding, more often than not, to the confusion, the guilt say, of a couple fighting, or a frightened old man barricading himself in against the landlord who wants to evict him. About this Duff I know nothing, save that he is a young man. He might be doped, drunk, fighting fit. And I, forty-three, fat, enervated these days, am in no shape to deal with any unruliness single-handed. Should I describe the singular, mortal feeling one gets in moments like these? Have we time? I'll say it's not so rare. Human enough. The ice in the gut, the inescapable sense of one's own cowardice and fear. It's the feeling I have now as I'm driving through the damp, half-alive town to find Duff. It makes me blush, even though I am alone.

The street I'm looking for is called Starway, an ironic enough name for a place where the locals say the muck rises from the cobbles to make the matter of the clouds on overcast days. I know the area only too well – the back-to-backs that straddle the hill and sell for a song, the thieving and the fighting, and the heartache of those trying to lead a decent life there. But I'm not thinking too charitably as I park the car at the end of the road, eyeing the kids who watch me lock it. This is one of those times when I crave a uniform, some manifest sign of authority. But then maybe these sophisticated mites, sentried about their lamp-post, recognize only too surely my shuffling gait, the typically shabby semblance of the social worker. They'll not feel threatened by me, I know, as I leave the car with one last exaggerated look inside for what might be missing on my return. I walk along the rime-powdered flags to number 15, pausing before the half-open door to offer a single defiant glance to the silent watchful group.

I do not bother to knock, since my instincts tell me that no one will answer if I do. Instead, I carefully push open the door with my foot, catching a zephyr of fruity urine from the darkened hallway within. I step inside and try the light switch even though I can see the bare wires poking from a hole in the ceiling. I shuffle a few crumpled boxes to one side with my knee and an empty bottle rolls away to the foot of the stairs. Scraps of newspaper, filthy clothing, old bike parts are jumbled everywhere, but it's nothing new to me. I've seen worse. Will see worse still, I'm thinking as I tap open the door to my right.

In this room I find an old man, the light from the street making him look spectral, the greasy dome of a bald head picked out as a white crescent above the purple mask of his face. He's lying on his side, staring into space as if he might already have crossed the celestial divide. And for his catafalque he has a soggy, crumpled sofa.

'I'm looking for a William Duff,' I say. 'D'you know him?'

But the old buffer just wriggles in his pit, loosing a fart in the mangy trousers. The eyes do not look at me, deliberately avoiding even my shadow which fills half the room. I take a deep breath, filtering the fetid air through my cupped hand. And get up close.

'Duff. Where is he?' I say loudly to the hairs in his ear.

'Get the fuck away! Go on with you! Leave a man in peace. For Christ's sake.'

His deep, rangy voice momentarily changes the character of the room, making it seem smaller. Then his body shudders with a monumental tic. He looks as if he's drying out. At the painful stage. A man, more than any other man, in need of a drink. I back off. There's no point in pushing him any further. He might get nasty. Do both of us some harm. And, besides, my business is not with him. No one has complained about his wretched state of affairs.

From an upstairs room comes a shuffling sound and a barking human voice. I leave the old one alone and tread with halting purpose up to the next floor where, in the front bedroom, in a numinous candlelight, I find someone I know. Old Wattsie. I say 'old' through habit as he is simply an old case, barely twenty-five, a chronic schizophrenic. He's sitting on a heap of rags and bursting cushions, looking flushed, boozed to the gills, smoking roll-ups no bigger than the matches he uses to light them. And yet, for all his obvious distractions – the compressed madcap laughter, the rhythmic patting of his head with one heavy palm, he, like the kids outside, needs to see no uniform to recognize me as a representative of some caring, meddlesome organization.

'Duff. William Duff. Do you know where he is?'

He thinks carefully. Nods. Shakes his head. Then his puzzled expression is shattered with green-toothed laughter. And I'm smiling myself, nodding in brief harmony with him, the moments crazed and empty with our failure to communicate.

'Duff?' he says, grinning. 'Duff duff duff. Hah!'

I wave in a gesture of resignation. This man, like the old one below, I shall also leave to the pleasures that divert him.

Crossing the landing, sending something small and scuttering away down the stairs, I open the only other door visible in the thin light.

And here I find my man.

The signs are good. Better than I'd hoped. At least he's had the wherewithal to make an old bedside light work – slight evidence that he has more about him than the down-and-outs with whom he's sharing the place.

He's sitting by the bare bulb of the light, raffia-blond hair in a flap over half his face, one leg tucked beneath him on a soughing stickback chair, the other wiggling to some tune in his head. He's wearing a grubby denim bomber jacket, baggy jeans, and a rag of a black T-shirt that bears the fading silver logo of a heavy metal band. He flicks the hair out of his face. Looks at me. Then he switches his attention back to some spot on the bare floorboards.

'There've been complaints. You're not meant to be here.'

Suddenly he jumps to his feet, making for the door behind me.

'Not now,' I say, halting him easily with my hand against his bony shoulder. 'Take it easy.'

He smiles faintly, the bottom lip dry and white over his big yellow teeth. Then he backs off a pace, standing awkwardly in the middle of the room, eyes half closed, waiting, it seems, for his next instruction. I take the initiative and point to a battered ottoman by the wall. He sits obediently, quickly folding his thin body into the angle between wall and seat. It's clear that he has no idea who I am and I'm thinking I'll not trouble myself to let him know. Not just now.

For effect, and for the true business of taking notes, I tug my diary from my mac pocket.

'This your address for the social?'

He strokes the down on his chin and nods, rapidly, as if the gesture is a rare luxury he's allowing himself.

'Well,' I say with a practised, careworn sigh, 'you're here illegally. Stay and you're in trouble. Better start thinking about some place you can go. D'you reckon?'

'Where? Where you gonna put me?' he asks, the voice unemphatic and scratchy, a transient flicker in his big eyes.

'Don't know. Won't be easy. No end of people looking for somewhere to live round here.'

His response is a goofy, incongruous grin, an expression my experience already tells me is the look of him – aloof, unconcerned, one of that breed of youths who have all the answers, the guardians of some particular secret, a trifle, a huge thing maybe, information they're going to retain, come what may.

'Family?'

He shakes his head.

I pause, examining him carefully from head to toe, an action designed to intimidate. Then I write my name and the address of the health centre on a page in the diary, scoring '10 a.m.' heavily at the bottom. I tear out the leaf and offer it like a traffic warden handing out a ticket, which I may well be as far as he's aware. He takes it with a detached submission, as if he's accepted that my assertions are to be his lot. As if, I'm thinking, he's been persecuted before.

'Don't look so bloody gloomy,' I say, clapping him on the shoulder. 'I'm not going to hurt you. I'm here to help. Just make sure you're at that address tomorrow morning.'

He looks quietly unimpressed now. Bored with me. Wanting me to go.

And I do leave, feeling my way down the dark staircase, whistling softly, quite convinced, as I step out on to the street, that he will not be at the health centre the next day, that I shall probably never see him again.

But the day has not done with me yet.

The car seems not to have suffered the attentions of the kids in the street whose cries and whoops I hear breaking on to the night air from a nearby alley.

I'm tired now and it's been an unfulfilling day, no problems solved, no cases I could say were complete and might be dispensed with. But then that's how it is in this job, cares and concerns, trials and burdens, all tangled up in one expanding muddle. I pull out on to the main road, watchful of the speeding joyriders of the night, the angry young men with their inexplicable, unbounded energy. I think about putting on the radio, for any kind of sound that might distract me, might help me loosen myself from the day. But even that seems too much of an effort and, besides, I should be home in less than five minutes. Then I shall watch the television, take a glass or two of the gin I'm partial to these days, just enough to induce sleep and the hope that I should wake refreshed for whatever the next day might bring.

The roads become quieter as I skirt around the town centre and head for the dim suburbs. Then I spot the social security building, the fluorescent lights still glaring out into the night. And beneath, pacing the pavement, is a figure I know.

I'm thinking I might pretend I haven't seen Malcolm, that I could easily slip away into the night. But he's standing half-way into the road, waving frantically. I pull round into the empty car-park and he follows behind, running up to the car. I wind down the window.

'What's up, Malcolm? Not still working, are you?'

'Th-there's this woman,' he says, leaning on the roof of the car, his breath swirling in white clouds.

'What woman?'

'Sh-she's in the s-social. C-caused a hell of a row. W-won't go home.'

'Have you seen her yet?'

'C-can't, Robert. J-just, can't manage it. Oh sh-shit, shit, what's the m-matter with me? I c-can't face it. It's t-too much. R-Robert, help me. P-please help me.'

He covers his face with his hands, looking as if he wants to weep, but nothing comes. I get out of the car. And for all that I like Malcolm, for all that I feel sorry for him, I want to pick him up and shake him.

'What do you want me to do?'

'I-I'll go in with you, R-Robert. It's my c-case. I t-took the call. B-but, I just can't do it on m-my own.'

I sigh ungenerously.

'It's a bit late for this carry-on.'

'I kn-know.'

'What's her name?'

'B-Bull. Angela Bull. Sh-she's . . .'

'Never mind. I'll work it out for myself. Go home, Malcolm. Get some sleep.'

He grabs my arm with a fearful solemnity.

'I'll c-come in with you.'

'It doesn't matter. What's another case?' I say, forcing a smile. 'We'll sort it out in the morning.'

'B-but what will R-Rycott say?'

'He won't know.'

'Oh J-Jesus, R-Robert. H-how will I be able to r-repay you?'

'Go, Malcolm.'

'Oh J-Jesus. Oh G-God.'

'Go.'

He looks at me with his eyes white and glaring. Then he

turns and makes his way, zig-zagging, across the spaces of the car-park. He stops at the entrance to give me one last look before he disappears, arms flailing, into the night.

I take a deep breath, trying to summon one more ounce of energy for this last unwanted task of the day. Perhaps I may well have to mention this to Rycott, if I can catch him in a sympathetic mood. But that will wait till tomorrow. A new dawn, I know only too well, can bring a very different perspective to things. Malcolm may be all right by then, though pigs, my professional instincts tell me, might fly.

The downstairs offices of the building are locked and in darkness and I follow the light up to the first floor. This is not a place I have ever liked, needing only to set foot through the door, to breathe in the fug of old cigarette smoke, to trample among the strewn plastic cups and leaflets to feel a sinking of the heart, to sense the air of woe and smarting confrontation that there is here.

The room is deserted save for a young woman, a girl, and a female clerk who is watching warily from behind a glass partition. The woman is pacing the floor, drawing sharply on a cigarette. She is small, hugging her thin waist, her eyes dark and screwed tight like insects on her pale, bony face. For some reason I think she has been screaming, but her anger is directed inward now while, next to the straggling rows of orange plastic chairs, the girl bites her nails, teases a few strands of her straight long hair behind her ears. She is sitting on a dump of stuffed black dustbin liners, bulging carrier bags and suitcases. She spots me first.

''E's here, Mam.'

The woman shakes a mass of brown hair from her forehead.

'And who the frig are you, then?' she asks.

'Mrs Bull?'

'It's Miss Bull. What're you gonna do for us?'

'My name's Bob Munro. I'm a social worker.'

'Oh bloody wonderful. A do-gooder. All I needed. Listen, I've told this lot and I'm tellin' you – it's no good sayin' we should go 'ome. We've got no bloody home. Not any more.'

'Well, if you want to tell me about it . . .'

'I'll tell you all right. Would you be goin' back for more of this?' she yells, pointing at a fresh glowing graze on her cheek. 'Or this?' she says, uninhibitedly ripping over the shoulder of her dress to reveal a hefty, ink-stain bruise. 'Friggin' wouldn't, would yer? But then how'd you know about it? Eh?'

Her features melt then, and tears follow, hard and cold. The clerk stirs in her seat, stifling a yawn, while the girl watches impassively, as if she's seen this display a hundred times before.

'All right,' I say. 'I think I get the picture.'

And already I'm picking up the bags full of shoes, coats, cardigans, everything I can manage. The girl jumps sprightly from the pile and begins helping me.

'Where you takin' us?'

'I can get you a bed for the night. It's all that matters for now, isn't it?'

She nods sapiently, lips firmed in agreement as the mother snatches a single bag from the pile and storms out of the room ahead of us. The clerk looks on, showing signs of neither gratitude nor relief as we stagger through the swing doors, down the stairs and out to the car-park.

'And what's your name?' I ask the girl as I begin heaving the bags into the boot.

'Sandra. Sandy, usually.'

'That's nice.'

'S'just a name, in't it?'

She throws her bags on to the back seat and climbs in beside them. The woman, Angela, is already sitting in the passenger seat, a fresh cigarette in her trembling fingers. 'Don't mind, do yer?' she says, waving the glowing red end under my nose.

'Be my guest. Wouldn't mind one myself, if you can spare it.'

She passes me a cigarette and I start the car.

With a gathering composure, Angela tells me a fragmentary,

familiar story. It's the boyfriend, see. He's a mean, possessive type. Handy with the fist. Doesn't need to get drunk to use it, either. They're the worst, aren't they? I mean, that's bloody sinister, she says. His name's Gary. Hasn't had a job for years. If she hadn't walked out of the flat, the council would have thrown them out. Owed bloody hundreds in rent. But that wasn't the real reason they went. Gary's home from the pub, this afternoon. Run out of money. And he's wanting his oats, isn't he? But she's not going to let him have it. Not like that. Not just when he feels like it. So he pulls a knife. Holds it to Sandy's throat. He'd have used it an' all. Crazy bastard. But Angela sorts it out. She's nice as pie. Gives him money so's he can go back to his mates. Every last penny she's got. So he clears off out again. Says he'll be back later for his dues, for what he reckons are his rights. So they're packing, grabbing everything they can carry. A neighbour says go to the social. They'll sort it out. They'll have to, won't they? The friend, a woman, gives them a lift there. And that's it. Angela'll not go back to Gary. Not ever. Not in a million frigging years.

I've heard it all before. Countless times. The formula always the same, almost tediously obvious in its telling. She'll probably be back with him before the week's out. Another woman of the town, this town, enmeshed in poverty, drawn to cruelty like a moth to a flame. I look in the rearview mirror at the girl who seems not to have been listening, sitting there, chewing gum, her blank expression intermittently lit by the headlights of passing traffic.

Soon we are at the refuge I have in mind for them, a house in a tall terraced row, the only place I can get them at this time of night. Angela stands in the doorway while I lug their things into the hall. She is quiet now, drained, damned by this day and the night. The lounge door opens and a bolus of television laughter accompanies one of the residents who appears with a clutch of empty coffee mugs. She smiles encouragingly at Angela but gets only a vapid glance in reply.

'You'll be all right here,' I say.

Angela sniffs, making a show of indifference.

'A choice, 'ave I?'

'Nope. It's this or a park bench.'

'Looks like it'll 'ave to do, then.'

She fumbles in her bag, producing the cigarette packet which is empty. She waves the thing around, not knowing what to do with it. I take it from her.

'I'll see if I can get you some. One of the other girls . . .'

'Don't trouble yerself.'

In this light she has a damp, masculine look, the look of the town. But she's not as confident as she would like me to believe, a little frightened, perhaps. And beside this fear I sense my own bulky male presence, a fleeting awareness of the physical power a man can hold over a woman. Then Kath, the warden, appears at the end of the hall, listening patiently to Sandy who's explaining, with expansive gestures, what has happened and why they are there. I should go and speak to Kath myself, but the weight of this long day is pressing down on me and I have yet to bring the rest of their things from the car. Sandy's testimony will do for now.

Angela is watching her daughter perform, smiling, an expression that adds years to her appearance.

'You've a good lass there,' I say.

'She's all right is Sand. She's fantastic. Don't know what I'd do without 'er.'

I bring in the last few bags, shuffling the heap a few feet further into the hall.

'I'll look in on you soon,' I say. 'See what I can sort out for you. It'll take time, I'm afraid. You've got yourself into a bit of a scrape.'

'Didn't bring all this on meself, fella.'

'No. Sorry. I didn't mean that.'

Sandy trips back down the hall.

'Her name's Kath. She says we can 'ave a double room. Single beds an' all.'

'Right, our kid,' says Angela. 'Best go view the accommodation, then.'

Angela clumps along the hall to shake hands with Kath

while Sandy watches her with a bold, matriarchal cast. Then the daughter turns to me.

'Ta,' she says. 'We're grateful. 'Onest we are.'

'It's what I get paid for. I'll get you fixed up with something more permanent. Soon as I can. If you think you'll need it, that is.'

'Oh, we will. Don't you go thinking that all she wants is a few days away from Gary. She'll not go back to 'im. Over my dead body.'

'That's good,' I say.

'Nah. We need a fresh start. We need somebody like you to 'elp us. You're a good bloke. Maybe you can 'elp us more than you think.'

'Sorry?'

But, while I'm puzzling over the remark, her adult mask disappears and she tugs at the lapel of my coat, pulling me down to kiss my cheek before she takes a step back, winking and grinning. 'Bye, Bob.' Then she's skipping off down the hall to where half a dozen residents have gathered to welcome the newcomers in tones of solace, reassurance. And Angela, central to the crowd, throws back her mane of hair, her shrill and catarrhal laughter rising high above the chattering noise.

Perhaps I should explain that there is no one out there looking for me, no detectives standing on street corners nervously fingering the bits and pieces of their hidden weapons, no constables going door to door, proffering photographs, asking, 'Have you seen him? The fat man? The murdering altruist?' It might make things simpler for me if that were the case. But it's not. While I write, while I dredge up the jetsam of this small life, it's in the certain knowledge that, as yet, I am suspected of nothing. All will change though, when I'm through with this, when I have either given myself up or crafted my own demise. It's down to me. And I should get on, for if I'm to furnish the whole chute properly . . .

It's the next day and I'm sitting in the office with the phone ringing and messages cluttering my desk and all the usual mayhem threatening to overwhelm me before the first hour of my work is over. At his desk Malcolm looks at his watch and slips a pill on to his tongue. He has mentioned nothing of the night before and I'm thinking I'll not trouble him with it.

I check my diary and try to rationalize my workload by eliminating all but the most pressing demands on my time. A disabled man's request for a bath hoist, for which I know I shall almost certainly be unable to wheedle the funds, can wait for another day. So too can a routine visit to a half-way house for the mentally handicapped. Then I find a note that has come my way from the doctor who visited Maisie Bertowski. He says he cannot find enough wrong with her to merit her admission to hospital. A social case, the scrawl says. But I find it hard to believe, thinking it more likely that he cannot find a bed for her. If I had the time today, if I were to do my job properly, I should go and find the fellow to press my opinion on the matter. Once I would have done just that. But these days . . . I'll let it slide for the moment: the doctor has asked that I look in on Maisie next week and that will have to do.

I make notes on the Bull woman, thinking I might leave her alone for a few days, by which time she'll probably have gone back to the boyfriend. After that I write up a new small file for Duff, presumptuously noting that he has not turned up for our appointment. Then it's ten thirty and if I'm to make any start on the day I must be away on my calls now.

The adjoining waiting room is filled with pregnant women, a couple of whom I know. I nod to them, hastening my passage before they can force any new problems on me. Then, outside, I find him, hands stuffed deep in bomber jacket pockets, the oily fringe swept behind an ear, eyes staring dully at the thin rain, mouth puckered about the tombstone teeth.

Let me say that I am not easily surprised by my clients. Once I step out of the health centre door my workplace is everywhere, on the streets, in every lounge and bedroom, on each park bench, in the bedsits, the hostels, the squats, the sewers, every blessed corner of this town. But this morning, at this moment, Duff, for some reason, startles me, wakens me from my complacency.

'You've come, then. I told you ten o'clock.'

'I was 'ere at ten.'

'So why didn't you come and find me?'

He says nothing, offering only that odd smile, a look of mild embarrassment.

There's a chance, I tell him, that I might be able to get him into Albert Hall, a rundown hotel that now functions as a place for the unemployed. I haven't been in touch with the landlord, but that won't matter. If there's a spare bed he'll be only too happy to fill it.

'Come on. We're going for a ride.'

Duff jerks himself from the wall with his elbows and trails me to the car.

When he gets in I have to prompt him with the seat belt. He tugs and fumbles with it, looking as if he might get angry. I fasten it for him, leaning across, smelling his citric breath, the damp in his clothes. He snuffles in my ear. Then we're away, slipping through the traffic in complete silence.

Ten minutes later and Ally, a Portuguese, the landlord of the hotel, is greeting us with his generous bevelled smile.

We are standing in the draughty reception area of this once handsome building, the air thick with cooking odours overlaid on the fusty hum from the damp walls and sagging floors. Duff seems quite uninterested in the place, hardly listening to Ally who tells us that he has a bed, though Duff will have to share the room with old Scotch Don, a kindly vagrant I brought here myself a fortnight ago. I say it sounds all right and I ask Ally to lead the way up the winding staircase.

'Bit cold up here, Ally,' I say.

'The heating,' he says, gesturing to the open spaces beyond the iron banister. 'Why waste it during the day? Costs a fucking fortune to run this place.'

On the attic landing, the cold tang of the staircase is replaced by a new pocketed smell of old male sweat, stronger in the room into which we earnestly troop. Duff eyes the dusty curling squares of carpet, the single ragged curtain that does not quite reach the sill of the gable window. There are two beds, two dining chairs, two chests of drawers – the absolute minimum requirements for clients of the social – and on the wall is a dingy Sunflowers print. Ally smiles, nipping the flesh on his chin, studying Duff like a farmer weighing up a cow at market.

'That'd be yours,' Ally says, thumbing at the bed nearest the window.

'What d'you reckon, Bill?' I say. 'Proper little palace, eh?'

He shuffles his weight from one foot to the other, stroking his chin as if in some subtle parody of the landlord.

'I'll sort it out with the social,' I tell Ally. 'Usual arrangements.'

'Sure, sure,' he says, still watching Duff. Then he adopts a serious frown and points at the boy. 'Listen. You bring no food and drink in here. You get breakfast and an evening meal and you're out of here between nine thirty in the morning and six at night. Come in drunk, start fighting, any of that shit, and you're out. Right?'

Duff smiles, offering no reply, dreamily scanning the four corners of the room as if looking for something.

'What about your clobber, Bill? We could go and get it now, if you like. You wouldn't mind, Ally, if we brought his things up this afternoon?'

'Nah. That'd be fine. Just fine,' he says, smiling again.

''Aven't got any things,' says Duff in a dry mumble.

'Well, that sorts that out, then,' I say.

Ally nods sagely. He knows all about this particular game. 'There's some old stuff in my cupboard downstairs. Maybe we could fix you up with something?'

But Duff offers only that odd glance, that look of boredom that he gave me last night in the moment before I left. And I'm glad of the hint, knowing my day is falling hopelessly behind schedule. Seconds later and we're going back down the stairs, Duff leading with his lolloping stride, the straw hair flying from his rounded shoulders.

In the reception area I give Ally a few hurried reassurances about the lad and about finances, but Duff is already out of the door. I chase down the steps and into the street, running to catch him up, needing to grip his arm to stop him. He seems to have forgotten me already, to have dismissed me from his existence with a facility that I'm beginning to find irritating.

'Where'll you go for the rest of the day?'

He shakes his head minutely, eyes big and empty.

'Look,' I say, 'I'm not the police. You can talk to me if you like. Won't cost anything. Are you going back to the squat?'

He thinks for a moment, wiping a droplet of rain from his nose.

'If I knew where you were going I could give you a lift. You'll get soaked just wandering the streets all day. Christ, Billy, say something to me.'

'I'm all right. I can manage.'

I sigh softly, letting go of his arm, my impatience receding. 'You'll go back to that room tonight?'

He nods once.

'You'd better. I can't fix it again if you don't. Those places are like gold dust. The Giros'll stop too, if you don't have a proper address. You're lucky . . .' But my words mean nothing to him. 'You're lucky.'

He has the flinching look of a wounded animal now and I'll not pester him further. I take a step back on the pavement, brushing some of the rain from my coat. Then I'm away to the car, looking round just once as he turns, walks a few yards back to the hotel, then turns again, shoulders hunched against the rain, resuming his original direction with no apparent rhyme or reason for his choice. I do not bother to pip my horn as I pass him. He has forgotten me already.

And I, too, forget him, as the day draws me on.

In the afternoon I'm attending a court hearing concerning the custody of a battered child. The parents, a sixteen-year-old girl and her thirty-five-year-old boyfriend, do not contest the judgement, supported by me, that they are unfit to look after the infant. They sit unmoving in the drab, drowsy court. Later, I see them on the steps outside, lighting cigarettes. The mother's hand shakes. She is close to tears. And the man looks at me, a familiar smeary scowl on his weathered face. 'Fuckin' do-gooder. 'Ow d'you sleep nights, eh?' And he snatches his girlfriend's hand and pulls her away, her heels clicking on the grimy flagstones.

Not ten minutes later and I'm stepping into a furious row between a newly released jailbird and his common-law wife.

[35]

They calm down instantly and the man's begging me not to mention this to his probation officer. I agree, for this one time. Any more outbursts like this though, and it's back inside, no messing. I leave them, quite certain that they will be at each other's throats again before I have reached the end of their street.

And then I'm away to accompany a woman who is being discharged from the town's mental hospital. We're to collect her three children from care. In the car she is pleasant, polite, composed. The stay seems to have done her the world of good. Is she looking forward to seeing the kids again? Can't wait, she says. She's missed them. They're all she's thought about these last three months. It's what's kept her going, the thought that they'll all soon be back together again. They'll make it work this time. It'll be good. Really good. Things have gone wrong in the past, she says. It's not her fault. It's just that she gets tired. Would I mind if she just had a little sleep now? I tell her that we're nearly there. She'd best rouse herself a bit. Then, as we pull on to the drive of the authority home, she really is asleep, snoring away. I can't quite believe my eyes. I stop the car and try to wake her. Then I'm driving again, fast as I dare, to the general hospital where they pump her stomach and tell me she's dropped enough Temazepam to flatten an ox. She must have done it just before I picked her up, they say. She'll come round soon. She'll live, says a nurse. Till the next time, I say. What did I mean by that? she asks. Do it once and as soon as things get tough again it becomes the only answer, I say. It's a game. A bridge once crossed, I add before I leave to face whatever else remains of this impossible, typical day.

'So what've you got for us? Ten-bedroom mansion? Bridal suite at t'Duke of York?'

'I'm afraid there's nothing doing at the moment. I told you, it takes time.'

'Just as well we like it 'ere, then,' Angela says, looking to Sandy who is perched on a cupboard, reading a magazine.

The kitchen of the refuge is alive with the slow bustle of the residents, washing up, making fresh additions to the endless stream of coffee mugs that make their way steaming to all points of the house. Angela has surprised me. I did not think she would have lasted here these five days. Rather, I genuinely believed that she might have let the boyfriend know where she was staying, half inviting him to grab her back. And she would have gone, offering only a symbolic, sullen resistance. It's the way with her kind, I thought. But she's proven me wrong so far.

She's sitting opposite me, her chin on one hand, the other flat against the scrubbed pine of the table. She looks bright enough, smiling, a tobacco fleck on an eye tooth. The daylight makes her look older than I had supposed, picking out the sharp lines on her temples, showing up the white puffy skin beneath her eyes. I'd put her age at about thirty-four, though she could well be younger, prematurely aged by a good seven years or more.

'You seem to be looking after yourself, anyway,' I say, folding away my diary. 'Had your hair done?'

[37]

'D'yer like it? Twelve pound fifty. Mario's. Up the precinct.'

'Looks good.'

'Ta.'

''Ey, Ange. You wanna watch our Bob,' says one of the women, struggling to keep her place at the crowded sink. 'Next thing 'e'll be askin' you out.'

'Might accept, an' all,' says Angela.

'Against the rules,' I say. 'Definitely no fraternizing with the clients.'

'Definitely no fraternizin',' she apes with a mocking solemnity, slapping her hand on the table top, the thin silver bracelets jangling on her wrist. 'What's your wife reckon about you comin' to a place like this, full of women?'

'All on 'is own, aren't yer Bob, darlin',' says another woman, drying suds from her red arms, coming over to pinch my cheek firmly. 'Aye, but you'd make somebody a decent 'usband, you would. Not like some o' the prats.'

'Too bloody right,' says the first woman.

Sandy looks up from her reading, seeming annoyed by this kind of talk. She shuffles down from the cupboard and leaves the room, sidestepping a freckle-faced baby on the floor. Angela watches her daughter go with a warm, concerned look.

'I have to be off now. I'll get on to the council. See what I can scrounge from the housing list. Can't promise much,' I say, standing and gathering my things together. 'So you're all right here for a while?'

'Snug as bugs.'

'I'll look in on you later in the week.'

'Can't wait.'

'See you.'

'An' you, Bob,' she says, with one eyebrow raised, her chin resting on her hand again. 'And you.'

Outside I find Sandy, sitting on a low wall in front of the house's big bay window, kicking idly at the stonework with the heels of her trainers.

'Shouldn't you be at school?' I ask.

''Alf-term. All week.'

'Sure?'

'Course I'm sure.'

She hops down from the wall and follows me to the car, watching as I shake myself out of my mac and drop it on the back seat.

'Why don't you do what they said?' she asks.

'Do what?'

'Ask Mam out.'

'Oh, I don't think so.'

'Go on. What 'arm could it do? She'd take to somebody like you. You'd be dead good for 'er. She's only ever 'ad bastards.'

'That right? And what'd make me so different?'

'You're a good man. A bleedin' saint. We both agreed.'

'Did you? Well that's all right, then.'

She trails me on to the road and round to the driver's side of the car. I get in and wind down the window to bid a perfunctory farewell.

'I'm goin' to fix a date for the both of you,' she says. ''77 Club. Tomorrow night. I'm off back in to tell 'er you'll meet there. Eight o'clock. No need to worry 'bout a babysitter. I've dozens to choose from. Eight o'clock. Think on. You won't let 'er down, will you? You can't, can you?'

'Sandra . . .'

But she has already gone, skipping back round the car, offering a V-sign to a passing motorist who has honked his horn at her flashing white legs.

The next day I have to spend the morning in the office, my turn to take the endless stream of calls that arrive for me and my overstretched colleagues. I find this more tiring than any other aspect of my work, preferring the streets to the health centre's arid air, the physical involvement with my clients to the impersonality of the telephone. Late into the morning there's a call from a husky-voiced man who will not give his name. He suspects a neighbour of sexually abusing his girlfriend's son. The man's done it before, he says. Done time for it, the bastard. Mightn't he have changed? I ask. Does a leopard change its fucking spots? he blusters. No, I say, our ungenerous philosophy suggests that it does not.

Come the afternoon, Malcolm has returned to the office, drained and edgy, and it's a relief to him when I suggest that he takes over my onerous duties while I attend to the anonymous caller's bidding. And I'm away then, driving through the town, smiling at its tumbling profile heaped beneath the blue convolutions of the distant moors, the cotton wool smoke from the liquorice factory, the sentry line of poplars that leads to the old Fourstones hospital, the spire of St Mary's reflected in the bronzed glass of a new insurance building, and I'm feeling that perhaps I can still love the place, that it yet has need of me and I am here and ready to respond to its callings. It's home. That's the word for it. My home.

Ten minutes later and I'm entering the tenement building the caller has told me about. I climb the stairs from the ground floor where the gases of passing traffic swirl with the accretions of litter. On each landing the sun filters finely through the dusty plate glass windows and from behind some of the doors I hear shards of arguments, a jig of rap beat, a single moan of lovemaking. Then I'm at the place I want. I knock gently on the lustreless paintwork of the door. No reply. I knock harder then, five times with my knuckle, the door-tap of a state official. Eventually there's a shuffling in the hall behind the door and a woman opens it.

She's holding a sleeping baby, looking half asleep herself, nuzzling the child with her pasty cheek.

'Mrs Wakefield?'

'Yeah.'

'I've come about your benefits.'

'What benefits? Who are you?'

'I'm here to check you're getting all you're entitled to. Complicated business these days. There's many don't get all they're due,' I say, smiling, though flustered by my own lying. 'Can I come in?'

She looks drawn, her body limp beneath the baggy shirt she's wearing over her dress, her bare legs and ankles thin and white. But a lumpen alertness is stirring beneath her vacant gaze.

'Where's Mrs Long? She usually deals with all that.'

'She's off sick,' I say, not knowing who she's talking about. 'She left a message for me to come and see you. May I come in, please? It'll not take long.'

A man's voice comes from one of the rooms inside.

'Who is it, Shaz?'

'A fella. Says 'e's from the social.'

'See 'im off, eh? There's a girl.'

She looks languidly into the hall then back at me.

'We're meant to be 'avin' our dinner soon. Can't you come another day?'

'I really do want to sort this out now, Mrs Wakefield.'

'What's 'e want, Shaz? 'E gone yet?' comes the voice. Then the man stirs heavily in one of the rooms and comes out to the door. 'What you after?'

'Like she says, I'm from the social.'

'Well, I don't think we need you right now. Got a job, see? Startin' Monday. Be signin' off tomorrow. So that's all right, in't it?'

He's about my age, balding, greying, a thin drooping moustache, but with an athletic build, muscles firm and rounded beneath his white vest. I have a split-second image of him playing football on a Saturday afternoon, relaxing with his mates over a few beers – things he will like to do, in this town where he belongs, where I am an outsider yet, for all my sentiments of just a few minutes before.

'Mr Wakefield?' I ask, fully aware that his real name is Peter Brittan, if my informant is to be believed.

'Doesn't live 'ere any more. 'Asn't been near in years. Mrs Long should've told you that,' says Wakefield, more awake now, manoeuvring the baby to her other shoulder.

'There. You 'eard that,' says Brittan with a smooth obstinacy, easing himself in front of the woman, placing one powerful arm against the door jamb.

I stare at him in my practised, concentrated way.

'Don't I know you from somewhere?'

'No, mate. Don't know you from friggin' Adam.'

'Funny,' I say, smiling. 'I could have sworn we'd come across each other some place.'

Across the landing a door opens six inches and a small old man peeks out.

'What you lookin' at?' Brittan says. 'You been told 'bout pokin' your nose into other people's business. You been told 'bout it before.'

The old man, who I guess is my anonymous caller, backs off and slowly and softly closes the door.

'I understand you have a son, Mrs Wakefield. He'll be about nine, isn't he?' I say, craning my head around Brittan's chest to catch her reaction.

'What's it to you?' she says, the baby sobbing into life in her arms. 'Listen, you 'aven't even told us who y'are. Not properly.'

'Yeah. That's right,' says Brittan. 'Where's your credentials?'

'I'm afraid I don't have any on me, though it's my duty to inform you . . .'

'Inform us what? Come on. Why're you really 'ere?' says Brittan, getting bolder, larger in the door frame.

And I cannot bring myself to say what I must – that there have been allegations, an anonymous call. It will need better planning, a more thorough and considered strategy. Brittan is a strong-looking man. I cannot handle this alone.

'All right,' I say. 'I'll go. There are a few points to check anyway.'

'That's right, pal. You go check yer points,' he says with a measured hostility.

I smile, nodding, backing slowly across the landing.

'I'll be back,' I say. 'Soon.'

'Just as you like. Whoever y'are,' he says, though we both know he recognizes me, as they so often do, for the profession I genuinely represent.

'Soon,' I say, turning to descend the stairs with a designed gravity in my expression and tread.

*   *   *

Come that evening and I'm tired, pondering the elaborateness, the sensitivity of this new case which I could well have done without. And I'm thinking it will have to wait until the morning, that I cannot quite face going back to the office and to Malcolm who I dare not trust with the details. But my sense of duty will not allow me to rest. I have achieved nothing this day and it seems I will only compound my failures by letting the Bull woman, Angela, down. Somewhere, in the mess of the morning, I had decided that she would probably not turn up anyway, having visions of her dashing with some fiery temper at the daughter and her scatty ideas. But I will go, out of curiosity, owing to a lifelong inability to let people down, because I have nothing to go home for anyway. If she comes, I will make my excuses, give her a lift back to the refuge and suffer the joshing ridicule of the residents to help her feel better. It's the best I can do.

So, it's eight o'clock and I'm standing beneath the flashing green and red lights of the 77 Club, feeling large and unlovely among the bright young things who brush past me, glad-eyed and hungry for the appalling electronic din inside the building. I walk a few yards along the pavement, catching my reflection in an empty shop window. Someone else looks back at me, a male frump in a grubby tweed jacket. He's fingering the knot in his wrinkled tie, frowning, out of place in this street at this time of night. He has things on his mind, a whole weight of mighty matters. He's alone. A lonely man with no pleasures he might arrange for himself here in this world of pleasures and the night. No talent for it. I rub my sore eyes, stroke the stubble on my chin, my thoughts so woolly now that if Angela were suddenly to appear I might not be able to speak a coherent sentence. A good ten minutes pass before I allow myself to believe, with growing relief, that she will not come now, that it's been a hoax all along. Glad of that. Glad I am, as I make my way back to the car-park behind the club. Then my heart shrinks a little as I see her running between the rows of cars, a wriggling, waving blur of colour, the flesh of her face made pale blue by the streetlights. She reaches me, laughing and coughing, clutching her slender white neck as she tries to get her breath.

Her appearance is a small shock – the short turquoise skirt and black tights, faded green blouse, a bulky pink jacket that the upper half of her body looks lost in. She rubs some itch on her nose and lights a cigarette, spitting out a mouthful of smoke between her violet-greased lips.

'We off then?'

'Where?'

'Up the club. That's the idea, in't it?'

In a corner of the car-park between a high wall and the fire exit of the club, a young man and woman are coiled about each other, writhing artlessly in the shadows, the light occasionally catching an arm, a bare leg, a half-turned self-regarding face. Not moving, feeling bloated with reluctance, indecision, I make a flapping gesture in their direction.

'My job, see. It's not my kind of thing.'

'All right. Let's go up the pub. Been in a pub before, 'aven't you?' she says with a fierce brightness, hooking her arm round mine.

'I'm not sure. I mean, I didn't really think you'd come.'

'Oh, cheer up, misery guts. We're gonna have a good time, aren't we?'

I can think of no excuse for a reply. An hour. It would fill the expectation. What harm could it do? And then the prevarications – a hard day, work in the morning. With a weary bewilderment I allow her to tug me on, back past the entrance of the 77 Club where three youths are arguing earnestly with a bouncer who will not let them in.

[45]

*   *   *

Soon we're at the Black Dog. She leads the way in like a schoolmistress or, yes, a rehabilitation officer, showing some recovering charge the way of the world, the places you must go to live a life, the efforts you must make. She orders a lager for herself and asks me what I want. I become flustered, fumbling for the coins in my trouser pockets, the landlord watching me, jowls heavy with mistrust.

'I'll get them.'

'No, you won't. It was my idea, this. I should buy the first round. S'courtesy. You get the next.'

Crumpled with timidity, a gaucheness I suddenly, acutely detest myself for, I allow her to pay. She picks up her lager and my own half of bitter and leads to a corner seat away from a huddle of men at the bar who pause in their dissolute conversation to watch her passing. Then they resume their talk, passing around fresh pints with a reverent solemnity as a juke box throbs into life, slow bass notes thumping into the corners of the otherwise empty room.

'Well,' says Angela. 'This is nice.'

I sip at the froth on my beer.

'So this was your idea, then?'

'Let's say it were more of a committee decision.'

'Do you consult Sandy on everything?'

'Most stuff. We share our lives, don't we? S'only fair.'

'Democratic.'

'Yeah. If you like,' she says, reaching under the table to scratch her ankle.

She lights another cigarette, blowing the smoke out between her teeth, smiling steelily.

'You're not used to this. I can tell.'

'No. I don't get out much.'

'Should. Does a body good.'

'Maybe it does,' I say, taking another drink.

'I want to know all about you,' she says, elbows on the table, chin cradled on her hand. 'I'm fascinated. Don't get many like you in your line o' work. They're all such stuck-up buggers, usually. You're different. Normal, like.'

'There's nothing much to say about me. You know the half of it already. I got divorced a while back. I'm a social worker. I live on my own. That's your lot,' I say, scoring a tactical point by taking one of her cigarettes from the packet on the table without asking her. 'Tell me about you. Bet your life's been much more interesting than mine.'

She laughs gustily.

'Want it for the records, d'yer?'

'No.'

'All right . . .'

She's a daughter of the town, she says. Her father worked down the pit. Took early retirement. Bad health. Died of pneumo-coney-whatsit a week after the place closed down. Hasn't seen her mother in years. Buggered off down south with some man, lorry driver from Rotherham. Angela bloody hated school. Hardly bothered turning up the last couple of years. Then she got a job in Woolies. Liked it. Good gang, plenty of laughs. She'd have liked to have stayed, seen if she couldn't make it to department manageress. They'd good as told her the job was hers for the asking. But then she got pregnant, didn't she? And the father'd cleared off to Saudi, hadn't he? Typical fella. Didn't get a penny from him. Bastard. Sandy's not met him. Not going to, either, if Angela's anything to do with it. Sod that idea about growing up and trying to find out who your real dad is. She knows half a dozen who've tried it. Never works out. Embarrassing. For everybody concerned. Anyway, she's pregnant with Sandy and her mother's taken up with this fella and she doesn't want her round the house spoiling everything and she says she's got herself into this mess and it's up to her to get out of it. She's a big girl now. A woman, like. So she gets this flat and she has Sandy and there's no one comes to visit her in the hospital. But she doesn't care. She takes the kid home and they're all right. She's no money. Not a frigging penny. But that doesn't seem to matter. Goes on like this for four or five years. Thought that was it for the rest of her days. Then along comes Gary. Seen him in the social. He's all right at first. Proper charmer, really. A looker too. Got no job, of course. But he helps with the bairn, decorates the flat. And she's wondering what she's been missing all these years. So he moves in. Seems logical. Why not? And it's all right at first. Lasts a good few years. But then he's wanting to know Angela's every movement. Has she told me this before? Well, she's telling me again. Needs to be said. Once he hit her and she fell bang into the enamel cooker. Ran off, didn't he? Didn't know what he'd done. Left her lying there on the floor all night long. She felt warm, peaceful, like it'd last for ever . . . Then it's morning and Sandy's up. She'd be only ten or eleven by then. And she's slapping Angela's face, fetching the neighbours, packing things she thought her mother'd need in hospital. What a kid. Eh? Angela's away for three days. Discharges herself in the end. Then she gets back and finds Gary waiting for her. He's sorry. He's crying. Horrible in a fella, that. So Angela's a soft cow, isn't she? She lets him stay, doesn't she? He's promised to mend his ways. But it only lasts till the next time. Then it's just like before, him demanding and creating, not letting her even go out to get the shopping. Went on for years. He wasn't always so bad and you sort of get used to how things are. But then there was the time he really flipped. The last time. That's the day I found her at the social.

I ask her if she shouldn't be thinking about pressing charges against Gary. I could help. But she says she'll not bother. Looks like he's got enough on his plate at the moment. Police have got him. Went mad when he found out she'd gone. Silly frigger tried to hold up a garage with a banana wrapped in a carrier bag. Can I believe it? she asks with her dusty laugh. Yes, I say. I can believe it. Gary'll do well, she says, if he comes up against that Judge Stockhill. Her mate's husband got him when he was done for housebreaking. The Domino Judge, they call him. Why's that? I ask. Because the only sentences he gives are either fives or threes.

The laughter comes from deep in her throat and I'm laughing with her. By now the pub has filled with a dozen or so customers and the landlord is smiling indulgently at us as he gathers our froth-choked glasses from the table. It's a look of friendliness I've rarely experienced of late, for all that I might visit in the pubs about the town. He does not see me as I am. I'm Angela's companion. Half a pair. Someone else . . . Then it seems no time at all before we're walking, quietly now, back to my car. The air has become sharp and the frost is arriving, dusting the pavement like crushed glass.

'It's been really good tonight,' Angela says. 'Best night out I've 'ad in ages.'

'Good. Glad to have been of service.'

''Ark at you. Been of service. You're not on duty now, you know. No. Really, you're dead easy to get to know. I can feel, well, sort of comfortable wi' you.'

'Unthreatened, you mean. That's all it is,' I say, as we pass under the pulsing lights of the 77 Club.

'Is it?'

'I'm not Gary. You'd be happy with anyone after him.'

'You should stop doin' yourself down,' she says, half serious, half distracted by the direction we are taking.

A few yards into the car-park and she's wheeling round the buttress of my middle-aged man's paunch. I see a liveliness in her, and a quiet irritation with my slowness, my puzzlement and maddening reluctance. She yanks my hand, pulling me towards the dark recess where, earlier, we saw the squirming couple. Another pair are there now, but they silently slink away at our approach, as if to make room for us, as if our names are next on some hidden roster.

'Angela?'

It's almost too real to bear, the touch of her skin, cool and clammy as if she retains the heat meanly inside her, in some secret organization within the skinny architecture. She pushes me up against the fire exit door, smiling in the dark, only her teeth visible, edged with a misty white. You're a good boy, Bobby. Every good boy deserves whatsits, she's saying, her words sprinkled with giggles. She's picked me for this moment, she says, guiding my fat shaking fingers inside her. My sweat

[49]

and her new, surface heat mingle in a curious acid. Something stirs in me, every part of me. A sea change. A rumbling in the blood. And I'm everyone I ever hoped to be, part of the town, all of it that I ever loved and admired, knowing, in an instant, all its secrets. Angela makes a cooing noise, designed to encourage me. Schematic. Scarcely believable. Though I want to believe in it. Yes, I do. And her hands and elbows and knees are everywhere, finding all my soft fleshy territory, that province so long untouched. What's Bobby doing getting a girl all hot and bothered like this? she's saying. It doesn't matter though. He can have anything he wants. He's a good boy. He's a bleeding saint, Bob is.

In my life I'll say there have been moments of genuine happiness, euphoria even. Revelation? Perhaps not. Though there
were times when I thought the veil had been rent aside, when
I thought I had glimpsed across the gap between this world
and the universe from which it was fashioned. Grand words, I
know. But it's the way I felt, perhaps in that moment at ten years
old when my mother said, for the only time I recall, that she
loved me (this for no act of my own 'kindness' – rather, it was
the day of my father's funeral, his demise having been a sudden
affair, a heart attack that genuinely shook us all). And probably
the day when I arrived in this town. Certainly that night when I
came back to this house and lay awake with my heart spinning
on a needle point, pounding like an adolescent's. What had
happened to me? Of course I had made love before, though
it was a long time ago and I'd never much cared for it, never
been so impressed (still, it had been on my mind of late). But
there was more to it than that. I was ready for being wanted.
Angela . . . I fell for her. Just like that. I'll call it love, if you
like. Though what was this love to be made of? What would
be its constituent parts? Touch. Optimism. I'll leave it at that.
Any more would bring us into the realms of sentiment. And
there's no room for that here. Not here. Not any place.

I digress. And there's no time for it. Best I stick to details,
to the proper order of things.

*　　*　　*

[51]

So it's the next day and I've slept for barely an hour, though it doesn't seem to matter – the energy I'd always felt I should conserve for my duties seemed there in abundance, available for any needy soul who might seek its use, anyone, even, in this room in the health centre where we are gathered for our weekly team meeting.

Of our quota of fourteen and a half social workers, just three of us are in attendance: myself, Malcolm, and Suzie, newly qualified and the newest member of our little society, our family (for that's how I'm seeing them, this morning. That's how much old cool, cynical Bob is secretly loving everyone in this hour. Though I've yet to put a name to it, yet to think it has any life beyond that one event of the night before.). Rycott is here too, on a rare visit, and he's listening to Suzie's tales of her recent holiday in Lanzarote, smiling indulgently, remarking expansively on the orange tan on her face and bare legs. Then, when it becomes apparent that no one else is going to show, Rycott stirs minutely on his chair, smoothing a crease in his trousers, a manicured fingertip fitted thoughtfully into the dimple in his small chin.

'I suppose you'll have seen last night's report in the local rag. About child abuse on the increase in our area?'

'Awful, that,' says Suzie. 'Why'd they go stirring things up like that? Just upsets people.'

'Well, I'm afraid', says Rycott, 'that it's an insinuation we must take notice of. If nothing else, it makes us look bad. And haven't we had enough of that lately?'

Malcolm wobbles, coughs and drops his notepad, picking it up again and realigning himself with one arm hooked behind his head, his legs sharply crossed.

'S-sorry, everyone.'

Rycott gives a polite killing smile and for myself I feel I should try and defend Malcolm, to raise some suitably couched objection to Rycott's pointlessly vindictive remark. But I can't. The words simply will not come. Rycott drones on again and I've said nothing since we began, doodling in my notebook, thinking again of last night, seeing, not the events, but a timeless, shapeless hovering, my heart rushing again with a little ache in the lower register of each rising beat. It's as if I'm someone else, unburdened, have become simply a fragile lightness, from my thick calves up to the top of my head. All of me. Is me. And I want to deny myself nothing of this intoxication, I'm thinking as I wake from the daydream to find the three of them looking at me, Rycott smiling coolly.

'Your case, Robert.'

'What?'

'I'm told you had a new referral. Yesterday.'

'That? Well, nothing much to go on. A neighbour's suspicious. That's about it.'

Rycott gives his tight smile of mild irritation. 'And do we know the man?'

'There's supposed to have been a previous conviction,' I say. 'Don't know the details, yet.'

'A history? Well, leopards and spots, eh? I think you'd best go round again, Robert. Let them feel your presence. And I want an update on all the others we've got on the books. That's one for you, Malcolm.'

'S-sure. Sure thing. I-I'll be s-straight on it. R-right away,' says Malcolm, slumping in his chair like a limp-stringed puppet.

'Good. Very good,' says Rycott. 'We need a well-formulated reply for the press. Can't have the buggers taking pot shots at us just when they feel like it. They need to know we're on the ball. We have to stand up for ourselves. Express ourselves. Sell our credibility. I think we all understand that. Don't we?'

Everyone nods in muted approval and Rycott leads us into the rest of the morning's business with talk of financing, budget problems, things that bore me, especially today. Eventually the subjects up for discussion become more diluted and local and the meeting breaks up. Rycott offers to walk Suzie down to her office at the far end of the building, leaving me and Malcolm who sits on the edge of his seat, looking forlornly at the floor, eyes round and suffering.

'Sh-shit, Robert.'

'I know.'

'Th-there's over t-two hundred cases. B-bastard's trying it on. He kn-knows it can't be done.'

'I'll help you. Not today. But I will help you.'

'H-he's a t-tough bastard, that Rycott. J-just thinking of his own s-skin.'

'You're right. But we won't let him get to us, will we?' I say, clapping Malcolm's shoulder as we leave the room. 'Life's too short. Look at what a beautiful day it is.'

'B-but it's p-pissing it down.'

'So? Who cares?' I say, laughing, holding open the door for Malcolm who slopes under my arm and away down the corridor.

Two hours later and I'm at the flat I visited the day before. This time the Wakefield woman lets me in with a weary groan and I follow her into the dim hall and through to the living room. She shoos a ginger tom from the fraying cushions of the settee and half-heartedly pushes away a few magazines, an invitation to sit down which I do not accept. Sitting at a table, scribbling animatedly in an exercise book, is the boy, a small kid for his age, wearing a grey school shirt and long black trousers. And in a chair by the fireplace, newspaper in his lap, feet resting on the hearth's cracked ivory tiles, is Brittan.

'You again, eh?' he says.

'Yes. Hah. Me again,' I reply, with a contrived lighthearted-ness. 'Now, about your Family Credit . . .'

'I thought I'd told you,' says Brittan. 'I got a job now. Got some standin'. Won't need your 'andouts any more.'

'You might not, Mr Brittan. But Mrs Wakefield here might.'

'Look,' says Wakefield, 'can you get on with whatever it is you've come about?'

'Right,' I say. And I begin making a few scarcely plausible arrangements for a review of her benefit claims, none of which I'm sure about, while I watch Brittan as carefully as I can, analysing the quality of his discomfort, an unease which causes him to rise stiffly from his chair. He goes over to the boy, leans over him, spreading his big hands flat on the table.

'Need any 'elp, Tom?'

'Nah,' the boy says irritably. 'I'm all right.'

'Y'know I'll help you any time you want it, don't yer, lad?'

'Leave me alone. I'm OK.'

I've stopped speaking and the woman is droning listlessly about the money she gets for the baby, the flat. 'I was thinkin' about askin' for something for clothes for meself . . .' But I'm not listening to her. Rather I'm watching the boy who seems to be shrinking under Brittan's close attention. Then he looks up at me, scowling sharply. Brittan stands in front of him so that I can see no more of this expression. But it's enough, a mere fraction of a second is all I need for my intuition to stir like an old wound. It's a hunch, an unscientific, inexplicable apprehension for which our profession is so often publicly calumniated, less famously praised when we get things right. But I'm sure, sure enough, that there is something going on here. The boy taps Brittan away with his arm and in the man's retreat, in the boy's new loaded glare, there are secrets, deceits, collusions. And I turn my gaze towards Brittan, giving him my half-smile, my clotted, troubled look.

'Y'know, I wish you'd get out of here,' Brittan says. Then he leaves the room in a tight, suppressed temper.

The Wakefield woman sweeps a few strands of greasy hair from her forehead, seeming to have noticed nothing untoward, looking near to falling asleep. I make a few thin-sounding arrangements about looking at her family needs and say I will call back soon. Then, I go over to the boy.

'Now then, Tom. Want to tell me a bit about yourself? Which school do you go to?'

But he's looking hard at me, eyebrows knitted under the fringe of brown hair. Slowly, he slides his fingers from the page of his book to reveal, in thick wavering pencil, the words 'Help me'. I back off, startled, some way between sudden elation at the affirmation of my suspicions and the dark prospect of what I must do next. He turns the page over and furiously begins drawing afresh. I turn to his mother.

'Not much of a talker, your lad.'

'No. Look, is there anythin' else you need to know?'

'Not a thing,' I say. 'I'll go now. But I will be back soon. Very soon. All right?'

She nods, yawning; shows me to the door.

Outside, the twilight is already arriving, the darkness beginning at street level, the cries of the newspaper sellers railing up from the shadows to the beauty of the dimming orange sky. I should be away now, straight back to the health centre, but the sweet little pains of this morning are with me again, and I experience them as something more defined and transitory, possessions that I cannot control, could easily lose. And beyond this understanding is a fear of this loss, a dark and heavy depression that might sweep it all away. Already, unforgivably, I have forgotten the call of my job, the poor mite's face that looked up at me with such dire, desperate need.

'Knew you'd come.'

'How could you know?'

'Sandy said same. She said you'd not be able to keep away after last night. Says we're meant for each other.'

'You told her? Everything?'

Angela laughs in the pale yellow light. Downstairs the television booms against the hum of the residents' low, halting conversations.

'So then, Robert Munro?'

'I've had a bad day. Awful. I need some company.'

'Thought you never needed anyone? Got it all sewn up. Your work an' that. S'all you want, you said.'

'Did I? I don't remember that.'

Angela laughs, tugs me across to the bed, her fingers pulling at my shirt.

[56]

'Poor Bobby's had a nasty day. Bobby want Angela make things better for him?'

'Not here. Please. I didn't come for that.'

'Oh shut up.'

'It's against the rules in a place like this. Strictly. What will the others say?'

'What'll they know?'

'Angela, I . . .'

'Shut it. It's going to be good. Everything's goin' to be all right. We're made for each other. We can be good for each other. Right?'

'If you say so,' I reply, feebly pressing my fingers about her waist, my reserve clumsily, wantonly consigned to some vague oblivion.

She snatches up my hands, licking and biting the fingers, forcing my palms against her breasts. 'Oh I say so, all right. I really, really do. And we're leavin' the light on. I want a good look at you, Bob Munro. I want to see what I've got. So don't bother askin' me to turn it off.'

It's corner-speaking time. The corner is in Rycott's capacious office. In the reception room beneath us we can hear phones ringing and doors squeaking. Rycott draws me further away from the hearing of his secretary who is sitting at her desk, scooping mouthfuls of lunch-time yoghurt, contemplating an apple on the piles of paper scattered about her typewriter. He looks at her with an unseeing eye, then turns to me again.

'You're sure?'

'Sure as I can be.'

'Sounds like the business. What more evidence could we need?'

'Maybe we could get to the boy at his school? A medical. Belt and braces approach,' I say.

'Don't think so. Not in this case. He might tell his mother, or that – what's his name?'

'Brittan.'

'Yes, him. Bloody animal. We don't want to give him the chance of doing a runner. He'll be in for a goodly stretch if we make this stick, and he'll know it. Could be tough on the kid if we hang around too long. No. It's the dawn raid on this one.'

I look towards the secretary, following the line of her gaze out of the window to the old oak tree in the health centre car-park. 'We'll have to be careful, John. Absolutely sure.'

'There's the court order to apply for, the police to be involved,' he says, wilfully ignoring my remark. 'A few days or so. I'll let you know. Meanwhile, mum's the word.'

He thinks deeply for a moment, hands joined like a suppli-
cant's. Then he smiles broadly and squeezes my shoulder.

'You've done well, Robert. I'm pleased. Proud.'

'I just hope we're right.'

'But we are. We're in the right. Has to be done. Don't look
so worried!' he says, guiding me past the dull attention of his
secretary to the door of the office. There he takes hold of my
shoulders again, as if about to embrace me. 'You look a bit done
in, fella.'

'A few late nights. You know.'

'Good. Glad to hear it. Anyone local?' he says, with an
irksome informal smile he reserves for the staff he favours.
We've known each other for five years, though I have never
really liked him, preferring to keep my distance whenever he
seemed to want to take me into his confidence.

'No. It's not that. Just work.'

'You work too hard, Bob. It's been noted.'

'Has it?'

'Look, why don't you take the afternoon off? I'm sure there's
nothing that can't wait. Let Malcolm do some of the donkey
work for a change.'

'Ah, I don't know. He's under a lot of pressure.'

'He has to shape up some time. We can't be carrying
passengers. Need to keep a tight ship, old son. No. You go
off. Enjoy yourself. Relax, Robert. Take it easy. You deserve it.
You've done well.'

'Done good?'

'Yes. Hah. That,' Rycott says, pausing thoughtfully for a
moment. 'It's what we're here for. What we do. Good. Now,
away with you. Home, Robert. I insist.'

So I drive away from the health centre, taking the suburban
route to my home. Rycott has rather thrown me by bestowing
this 'favour'. I have no talent for relaxation, for leisure, though
I might have enjoyed the time off if I could have anticipated
it. I might fetch my groceries from the supermarket, but that

would leave another hole in the week, or I might busy myself about the house, though I have never had any inclination to decorate, plumb, trouble my mind with the various tasks that men use to divert themselves. And I have so few friends, never seemed to want for them, it's true. The hours will be long and empty and wasted, I'm thinking. I had already planned this day, as I plan all my days, and I was to work solidly through to the evening to induce a torpor that would keep me from thinking about Angela. For now she is a presence in my life, an indisputable fact, and to test the worth of my feelings for her I must resist seeing her for a while, to allow whatever part of me has become excited by her to reveal its true shape and nature. But I'm wanting her, I'm needing her touch now as I reach my street and continue on past the end without thinking. Then I'm out on the main drag into town, completely directionless, almost allowing the car to drive itself, to wish it could make my decisions for me, following only the most convenient lines of traffic, the left turns, the through lanes, till I'm stuck behind a dusty green council van which I follow out of idleness, out of a silly whim of fate. If it leads me to the refuge then it is right that I should go there today. It slows at a roundabout indeed near the area of the house, nosing out, the driver uncertain which road to take. My heart leaps a little, deliciously so, and I have my bumper almost touching his. Then the driver indicates left at the second turning, gathers speed with a cumulus of fumes from the van's exhaust, and I'm after him, away over the river, past St Mary's, till he pulls over and into the library car-park. I pull up beside him and get out. Here, back near the town centre, I'm at least three miles from the refuge. The driver, a mud-spattered workman, gets out of his van, looking hard at me.

'You been followin' me, pal?'

'Yes,' I say, smiling. 'I have.'

'Time an' motion?'

'No.'

'So what's the idea then?'

'Fate,' I say, without thinking. 'Oh, nothing. I'm sorry.'

He tugs his bag of tools from the van's passenger seat and slides the door to with a clatter, looking at me with the picaresque sneer that the men of this town reserve for milksop professionals such as myself. 'Headcase,' he says as he brushes past me and away behind the library.

Subdued now, I lock the car and begin walking aimlessly towards the town centre, fearing to analyse my reasons for being here, the little madness that has possessed me in these last few minutes.

And among the trudging shoppers, the sharp-eyed street corner dealers, the darting, truant-playing children, I'm still not sure of myself, still feeling large and quiet and isolated as if I'm only half here, as if the rest of me is elsewhere in this town, owned by someone else. I shamble along, into an arcade, staring at a shop window full of little artefacts, porcelain butterflies, sticks of incense, pen tidies, hand-carved wooden elephants, things I would never buy, could never want. All this life teeming around me and I know nothing of it, take part in hardly any of it, save for its worst side, the festering core where I ply my trade. I walk on, irritated with myself, angry with Rycott for giving me this time which I could have used more usefully. Then, out in the grey light of day, leaning against the wall of a bank, is a figure I recognize, someone I'd largely forgotten about.

He's looking down at the pavement, then to his side, then straight at me. When he sees that I have noticed him, Duff slides his hands up from his trouser pockets to the slits in the side of his jacket. I get the curious feeling that he has been there for a long time, waiting for me, perhaps, though my approach, my lessening of the space between us, seems to make him wince with unease.

'Bill? How's tricks?'

'All right.'

'Still in the digs?'

He nods once.

I look at my watch, cheered by the fact that the afternoon is passing, and that I may have found someone with whom I might be able to recover my sense of duty, a client in whose company I could lay waste another hour.

'Listen,' I say. 'The job shop's round the corner. Should still be open. Fancy a wander?'

'Don't mind,' he says, these two words sonorous with indifference, though he's away already. I trail after him, already feeling better – an arriving sense of purpose, a little sanity regained.

In the Job Centre we stand beneath the soft hum of the fluorescent lights, staring at the cards arranged on the boards like a patchy stamp collection. Plasterer. Lathe Operator. Chocolate shop assistant – overall provided. Driver: HGV Class II. Nursery nurse.

'Butcher, baker, candlestick maker. Everything but the Pope, eh?' I say.

But Duff is simply watching the cards. I wonder if he can read.

I draw him towards the 'No Experience Required' section then leave his side to amble down the room, quite certain that most, if not all, of the jobs on offer are beyond what the lad's capabilities might be. At a desk in one of the cubicles a woman asks a young man for the details of his working life. He's smiling at her, says she can have all the details about him that she wants, starting with the fact that he's free tonight. She asks drily if he can remember his national insurance number, if he can carry big numbers like that in his head. I wander back, finding Duff looking round him like a thief with an eye for anything he might steal.

'Well?'

'Nah,' he says, with a goofy grin which fades quickly to a cold nothing.

'OK. How about a coffee? There's a place next door.'

I lead the way without waiting for a reply, not even looking to see if he's following until we are in the café. There I turn to see that he is already seated, having chosen the first table by the door even though the place is empty. I go to the counter

[63]

and return with two slopping coffees, cigarettes, and a thick cream éclair.

'That's for you,' I say, sliding the cake across to him. 'You'll not get much by way of sweet stuff with old Ally. Money won't stretch to it. He's a good sort, though, your landlord. Plenty worse.'

He picks up the cake and bites slowly into it, the cream oozing through his fingers. I light a cigarette and just watch him, feeling like a father who's brought his kiddie up the town for a treat. When he's finished, I offer him a serviette which he eyes suspiciously before taking it from me and wiping his mouth. Then he screws the thing up, rubbing his lips once more with the back of his hand.

'You don't say much, Billy. Don't you like talking? Most people like to talk about themselves if they think they've got an audience. Christ,' I say smiling, 'I don't even know where you come from. I'm supposed to have all that for my notes. Have you any family round here?'

'No.'

'So where'd you spring from? Who brought you up? Some-one must have?'

'There's nob'dy round here. Nobody, any place,' he says, licking his teeth with his tongue.

I laugh emptily. 'Well, I don't know . . .' Then I begin lecturing him weakly about looking for a job, finding a permanent home, suggesting, with some exasperation over his silence, that he has to do something with his time on this earth. 'What do you want from life? Everybody's looking for something. No?'

He looks at the door, half turning towards it, then he smiles in a controlled, fierce way that I've not seen before. 'I want to kill somebody.'

Across the room the girl who served me drops a tray laden with crockery. It's a weird response, perhaps telepathically evoked, for she cannot have heard what the boy has said. For myself, I'm smiling, wide-eyed with genuine surprise.

'You want to what? Did I hear you right?'

[64]

'Can we go now?' he says, making to leave his seat, the face set sullen once more.

'No. Wait. Let me get this right. You say you want to kill someone?'

'Told you what you asked. Now I want to go.'

'Oh come on, Billy. I want to know. Have you anyone particular in mind?' I ask, smiling still with a heady disbelief.

But he's standing now, already making for the door.

'Hang on! I'll give you a lift.'

I catch him on the street corner.

'Let me take you back to the hotel. You don't have to tell me anything you don't want to.'

Five minutes later and I'm driving through the late afternoon traffic. It takes another fifteen minutes to get to the hotel, a time when we do not exchange a word, when I'm feeling awake, more my old self for the first time today. I'm itching to ask him about his extraordinary statement – it hangs between us, solid and immovable – and I'm thinking I might follow him into the hotel and corner him until he's explained himself. But when we've arrived he untangles his body from the seat belt and is away up the steps like a mountain goat. By the time I get into the building, standing breathless in the reception area, he has already disappeared up to his room. Ally comes out of his steamy kitchen, wiping his hands on a cloth, casting a glance up the staircase.

'Queer fish, your lad. Doesn't say much.'

'I know,' I say, wiping the sweat from my forehead. 'Is he, well, behaving himself?'

'Good as gold. No trouble. I'll take a few more like him, if you've got them. I like them quiet.'

I shake my head, looking up the staircase myself, deciding then against the idea of following Duff to his lair. 'No. No more like him,' I say, turning to leave.

A few minutes later and I'm driving home, the sun already down, the streetlights glowing and glowing against the night that stretches long and empty before me.

'They're pulling that lot down soon.'

I gesture at the row of houses I can see through the grimy glass of the window. The roofs of two of them have lost their slates, the black joists open to the sky. In a yard below, a woman is hanging out washing, pegs held in her mouth. She picks towels and baby clothes from a basket, shaking them out and fixing them to the line.

'It's B an' B,' says Angela. 'We want a proper 'ome. Like the one we had.'

'I know. And I'll get you a place. Soon as I can. It's just that there's nothing doing at the moment.'

'We'll stay as we are, then.'

'There's a limit to the time you can spend at the refuge. I really don't have much influence in those places.'

I walk about the small room, around the two beds covered with faded pink eiderdowns. At the tiny sink I try the taps, then I knock at the door frame and slap the walls with my palm, humming with an unconvincing satisfaction as I stride in measured paces back to the window. 'You could soon fix it up. A few of your own things in here and it'll seem a lot more cheerful.'

But she's not listening. Her face has darkened, browned beneath the violet blusher, an ivory shadow spreading past the hairline. She tucks a loose corner of her blouse into her jeans, looking puzzled.

'I thought you were gonna help us, Bob. Do us a favour. Thought we were special to you.'

'And you are, Angela. Really you are. I'm doing my damned-est, honestly. It's just not that easy.'

She draws her lips into a tight knot, eyebrows gathered in a studying frown.

For the past half an hour, the time it took me to collect Angela from the refuge and bring her here, there has been no mention of our earlier meetings, tumblings, call them what I might. She was breezy, pleasant enough on our way here, but the sight of this place, the rubbish piled on the doorstep, the monotonous, world-weary tone of the landlady, flattened her mood in seconds. And I'm wondering what real value I have for her, whether our affair – if that can possibly be the word for it – is not already over, has scarcely had a life at all. I'm blushing at the thought, standing perfectly still now in the enclosed silence of this, yes, dispiriting little room.

'I could visit you here,' I say, sheepishly.

'S'B an' B. Not big enough to swing a cat.'

'But Angela . . .' I begin, though I'm interrupted by the landlady who appears, standing in the doorway, cigarette in one hand and a Yale key hanging from a length of string in the other.

'Well?' asks the landlady.

'Angela?' But she looks away, rubbing the smooth skin of her neck, awaiting my verdict. And I pause, thinking for a moment, seeing Angela's flinching expression. Daughter of the town. Scapegoat for its failures.

'No good,' I say. 'Not quite big enough. Sorry, and all that.'

'No need to feel sorry, fella. It's no palace, I know, love,' says the landlady, turning to Angela. 'But there's plenty others'll be only too glad of a room like this. It's not everyone can afford to be fussy.'

Angela picks uncomfortably at the strap of her handbag, biting her bottom lip.

'Well, we'll go. Shall we, Angela?'

She sweeps past me, leading the way out, her turn to blush as she skims smartly past the landlady and off down the stairs.

In the car she is radiant, enlivened again.

[68]

'Knew you wouldn't let me down. You couldn't really 'ave thought me and Sandy'd stay in a dump like that. Could you?'

'It's not what I think. I know it's a dump, but it's about all there is. You're in no position to be choosy.'

'Come on, Bob. Stop takin' it so seriously. That's your trouble. You take everythin' personal.'

'You hardly know me.'

'I know enough,' she says, putting her arm around my shoulders, her damp breath in my ear as she kisses my neck.

'Angela. Please.'

'Anyway,' she says, pulling away. 'You told me plenty about yourself the other night.'

'I told you no such thing. There's nothing to tell about me.'

'Well, there y'are then. If there's nothin' to tell, then I know all there is to know,' she says, laughing with an infantile satisfaction.

At a red light she sucks two cigarettes into life, passing one over to me.

'Where we goin' now?'

'Back to the refuge. Where else?'

She tuts sulkily. 'Don't feel like goin' back there. There's nothin' to do. They're a miserable lot, some of them women. All they talk about is 'ow much they hate men. Gets borin'. Where you goin' now?'

'I've one more call to make, then I'll get lunch some place.'

'What? At your house?'

'I hardly ever go home during the day.'

'Oh, go on. Let's go to your place. I'd love to see where somebody like you lives.'

'I'm a busy man, Angela,' I say, trying to concentrate on pulling out at a junction. 'I've things to do. People expecting me.'

'Give over. Bet there's nobody you can't put off for 'alf an hour. Go on. Live dangerously. I've been tryin' to imagine what your house'd be like. I'm dead curious.'

'Angela . . .'

'Bob. Please?' she wheedles. 'Pretty please?'

At the end of my street there is a closed-down garage, white paint peeling from the walls, layers of handbills pasted on the boarded-up windows, thistles sprouting from cracks in the forecourt. I'm turning past it two minutes later, a little heat inside me, a sense of deceit for which I feel no shame. Hadn't I already decided that she might come round to my house before the thought even entered her own little head? Was there, is there something in my blood that's making these decisions for me? And for all my circumvention, my words to the contrary, didn't I secretly want her to turn the bedsit down? I can scarcely bear the thought, wondering only how I am to control myself, what new embarrassments may be coming my way.

In the house she is singularly still, tacit, seeming limited in some way. She watches me in the kitchen as I make tea, scouring the cupboards for anything I might be able to offer her for lunch.

'It's just 'ow I pictured you to be. Domesticated. Better'n a woman.'

She has a look of smiling bemusement and I'm fearing some small ridicule. But she's not quite up to it, doesn't know the rules here. I wave a packet of digestive biscuits at her. She nods and we go through to the lounge where she occupies one armchair and I the other. I put the tray of tea on the floor between us.

'S'nice. Nice place. 'Omely.'

Her last word surprises me and I join her in looking about the room, as if I'm a visitor myself, eyeing afresh the drab furniture, the lumpen sofa, the yellowing paintwork, the rows of books that I haven't read for sixteen years, the grimy Wedgwood vase on the mantelpiece, the little glass dish in which I keep my spare change. An old wound stabs and stirs as I remember the brief optimism that went with the buying of some of these things, when I first came here with Caroline. Since she left I've not improved the place at all.

'Could do with decorating,' I say. 'And the windows need replacing. Fancied those plastic-framed things. But I never seem to get round to it. You don't notice things so much when you're on your own.'

'Wouldn't change it. Not a thing,' she says, slipping languorously from her chair to the floor to pour the tea. Then she sits back against the cushions of the chair, smoothing a little chaos of hair behind an ear, looking almost unbearably soft and reflective. She asks me about Caroline and I tell her it was a hopeless business, that we weren't really suited. I begin to lie, saying that Caroline wanted material possessions, things I wouldn't have known how to provide, even if I'd won the pools. And I tell her of my two brief dalliances with women since then, expanding and exaggerating the details, perhaps to hide the truth of my long solitude. Then I stop the conversation, despising myself for my deceptions, the pointless hostility of the details, thinking that Angela probably doesn't believe the half of it anyway. A silence follows in which she passes me my cup, a tiny, informal gesture which seems to embarrass us both.

'Well,' she says. 'This is nice.'

Now I can hardly help myself, setting the cup in the hearth, slithering clumsily to the floor beside her, my knees crackling. She watches me with a fragile, sagely smile, as if she's had this approach a thousand times before, as if – dare I believe it? – this is what she wants me to do. 'You,' is all I can say, a stupid word, but the coolness between us is replaced by a hunger in the air, in the ancient, bewitching code I feel in her fingertips as she slips her hand beneath my shirt and squeezes the flesh of my stomach.

'I'm fat.'

'Love 'andles. That's what these are.'

I try to kiss her, but she holds me off.

'Not 'ere,' she says. 'Upstairs. Now.'

She takes my hand and leads me out of the room to the stairs.

[71]

There she shakes herself loose and skips up, seeming more sure about where she is going than I, an utter stranger now in my own house. In the bedroom she is already undressing, quickly, unfussily. It's a personal, ordinary ritual she's used to, like painting her nails, blowing her nose. As I'm taking off my own clothes, shedding any reserve I might have had with each item, I'm watching her, the revelation of her skin, the uncovering of some badly kept secret that once again I must have in the open. She complains that the room is cold, shivering, though I'm wondering if she might actually be embarrassed, which intrigues and excites me. Then, when she is in the bed waiting for me, there's a look in which we connect, a moment yet sustained when I'm climbing in beside her, to take her without ceremony. I should respect her vulnerability, tread carefully in her territory. But I can't stop. 'Nice. Steady,' she says in a rasping whisper of her street voice. Deep. Slow. Hot. In my mind there's another picture of her, in another bed with her last lover, whoever that might have been, whenever it might have been. And it makes it better. She rolls her hips against me as if wriggling into some tight-fitting garment. Soft. Good. 'So good,' she says.

It's an age later, though no more than half an hour, when she's lying in the crook of my arm, her skin warm and smelling of the soap she must have used that morning. We're sharing a cigarette, using a tissue to gather the ash, and her clothes are scattered about my bedroom floor, blouse and jeans, the cloudy tangle of her tights, foreign things, discarded obstructions to her living flesh. And I'm wanting to ask her the obvious, that I'd like her to come and live with me. Sandy can have the back bedroom. But the words are lodged in my head and have been for too long – if I were to say these things now, the sentences would be artificial, as if I had made them with my hands and pinned them on the air. I can only say the opposite of what I want to say, that she must be going soon, that I've work to do, not the least of my tasks being to try and find her a place of her own. She slips from the bed to the bathroom, and I look awkwardly around for somewhere to put the finished cigarette. Her absence fills me with a sense of loss, my true wishes in an icy, fulsome abeyance.

When she returns she begins dressing, slipping a slender, calloused heel through the leg of her pants. She asks me to help with her bra, though she can't need me to – it's a kindness, a nicety, a treat for the boy. And I feel far from embarrassed by my own nudity, seeming to want to test her with it, offering my unattractiveness for her disapproval. Maybe that's what I'm after, to have her leave me like this, defeated, victimized. She buttons her blouse, rolls her jeans over her thighs with a giggle, bundles up the tights and jams them in her pocket. Then she comes over to me, resting her arms on my shoulders, rubbing her nose against mine.

'I think we'll move in tomorrow. Any objections?'

I pull her hands down, holding them between us. This is not a time for tenderness. Rather, it's a pivotal moment, a second of silence to allow the arrival of a decision. Footsteps pass quickly along the pavement beneath the window. A car is started and pulls away down the street. There are no thoughts in my head. Whatever comes out of my mouth, that independent organ over which I now have no control, will be the right choice.

'No,' it says. 'No objections.'

The next day, I brought them.

All night long I'd hardly slept, though there were no second thoughts, no curiosity for the end of my solitude, my long and, yes, lonely years. At nine o'clock I rang Rycott and asked for the morning off, which he agreed to without hesitation. I did not explain why and it didn't seem to matter. Then I tidied around a bit, vainly trying to air the bed in the spare room which had not been slept in since I entertained a male colleague from Lancashire, here on some research project, years ago. The mattress had a fruity smell which I tried to brush away. Then I dampened it with a cloth, turning it over and back again until I was in a small panic over the thing. I found the newest sheets I possessed – dark brown ones, at least ten years old – and folded them tight over the mattress, hoping that would do. And then I brought them and the house seemed suddenly noisy, inevitably smaller.

I bring the carrier bags in a one-man relay while Sandy struggles up the stairs with a huge suitcase. I follow her up to the room.

'I'll paint it. Soon as we're straight,' I say.

'S'no bother. It's fine. Really,' she says, arranging T-shirts, jeans, shoes, underwear, in little dumps about the floor. Then she lifts a block of white linen from the bottom of the case. 'I'll put these on,' she says, expertly throwing open the sheets so that they unravel flat on the bed. 'I always sleep in white. Don't mind, d'you?'

'No. Of course I don't mind.'

Angela comes shuffling up to the small landing with a bulging pink shopping bag and, under her arm, a huge good luck card from the girls at the refuge. I follow her into the bedroom I am now to share with her (an arrangement we have come to without any exchange of words). She says, with a tetchiness that concerns me, that the wardrobe is too small. I laugh nervously, momentarily abashed. I tell her I'll get a new wardrobe, big as the room. 'So there'll be no space for us, stupid,' she says, still cool, tired perhaps. Then, from Sandy's room, comes the sound of a radio, filling the house with a swirling electronic wail that its old walls and rafters can never have suffered before. Angela seems not to have noticed the noise, seeming to find it quite natural, to relax now in her unpacking efforts, going into Sandy's room to exchange some low inaudible words with her daughter. She returns smiling, as if the recipient of a recent joke.

'Well, I'll be off,' I say. 'Work to do, and all that.'

'All right, Bob,' she says, now pulling back the covers on my, our bed.

'See you later, then.'

'Yeah. Later,' she says, her back to me as she concentrates on her task of rolling up the sheets into a ball and tossing them into a corner.

Within fifteen minutes I'm alone in the health centre office, a good hour earlier than I had intended. I pull Angela's case file from the cabinet, and see that I have not made a single entry since the day after I found them both at the social security building. And I write nothing now, leaving her address as before, toying with the idea of destroying the document, then settling for dropping it beneath a heap of old notes in the drawer of my desk. I sit back in a reflective mood, trying to force into my mind the fact that there is now someone else in my house, making their home among my furniture, the belongings which I called my own, but which now seem to possess a strangely temporal quality. And these feelings become directly connected to my time with Caroline, bringing a fresh awareness of myself, a new, younger identity which reduces the years in between, makes them seem no more than a time of waiting, as if they did not exist at all.

Later in the day I'm driving to the outskirts of town. At my side is Duff, silent as ever. We are going to the Royfix light industrial unit, a workshop for the disadvantaged – the blind, the limbless, the mentally ill (an unfortunate mix, I know) – and I have it in mind to ask if they might be interested in taking on Duff, though he's hardly qualified for the place, unless you could call his annoying inertia a mental defect. In truth, I don't have to take this kind of interest in him and I'm sure he would be happier, since he seems to want for nothing and no one, if I just let him be. But then it's probably that which keeps me going with him. His reticence charms, his idleness is irksome. And he's young, so young. Then there's the matter of his weird outburst in the café. There may be something in that, enough, perhaps, to warrant my continued interest in him.

'So what's new, William? Done anyone in yet?'

'Eh?'

'You know. What you said that time, about wanting to kill someone?' I say with a chuckle.

But he remains sullen, unknowable, and we say nothing more until we have reached our destination.

The estate is a new complex of cheery, cream-bricked factories, aluminium warehouses, glass-fronted offices. I park next to the only other car outside the Royfix building and Duff follows me like a bored mongrel to the double glass doors. He hasn't the remotest idea why we are here since I gave only scant clues, thinking he might run off if he had any time to consider the prospect of having a job. I hold open the door and chivvy him inside.

In the office by the door, the manager, Jack Healson, stops eating the heavy cooked lunch on his desk, wipes grease from his lips with the cuff of his overall, and comes out to greet us. I introduce Duff and Healson extends his hand, a gesture which makes Duff smirk before he tenders his own limp fingers in the slightest excuse of a handshake.

'Pleased to meet you, Billy,' says Healson. 'Bob's told me some things about you. All good.'

Duff's smile is minutely revived before it melts with a tic of the cheek.

Healson leads the way, Duff shuffling along, changing his legs to keep pace as we march briskly along the corridors, past closed doors from behind which come various thin sounds of machine and human activity. At the end of the building Healson shows us into a room where a handful of men and women are seated around a big table spread with heaps of electronic jewellery. Nearest to the door a blind man in dark glasses attends to a tiny cube of wires with minute, almost imperceptible movements of his fingertips. Beside him an old woman is smoking and scowling, seeming to have had enough for the day. 'Circuit boards,' explains Healson. 'Fix 'em up for the army.' He turns to Duff. 'Bob tells me you're bright, Billy Duff. Fancy a go at something like this?'

Duff inspects the boxes of transistors, resistors, the bushy tangles of hair-thin wires, eyeing it all with a silent, doleful disregard.

'Well, I think you could give it a try, eh William?' I say.

He sniffs drily, saying nothing, looking as if he could wilfully fall asleep where he's standing. Then suddenly the arid workshop air is split by a piercing shriek and one of the men is on his feet, his chair clattering behind him. 'Oy! Yous'll not talk to me like that. Bastards!' he's yelling to the ceiling. 'I'll fucking have you for that. 'Ave you for it!' he bawls, shaking his fists in an unfocused rage, the brilliantined head shaking, his bright red tie swinging as he rants and screams. The blind man wearily tells him to shut up. And indeed he does, as suddenly as he began, giving the plate glass window behind him one thudding slap before recovering his seat and resuming his work with a wide moist grin.

Healson studies Duff's reaction, but the lad, unlike me with my thumping heart, seems quite unmoved by the outburst. Perhaps he's been in a place like this before? Psychiatric hospital? Bad boys' school? Healson's smiling. He's already made his mind up about Duff, a knowing eye spotting the characteristic indifference of the institutionalized. 'Don't you go worrying about Alan,' says the manager. 'He's harmless. Just bleeding crackers. That's all, isn't it, Al?'

'Too bloody right, Mr Healson,' says Alan, licking the sweat from his top lip. 'Must be, workin' for these wages.'

'Peanuts,' says the chain-smoking woman. 'You pay peanuts an' you get monkeys workin' for you.'

A melancholic laughter circulates unevenly around the table.

I tug Duff to one side.

'What do you reckon? Seem like a decent bunch. Yes?'

The big yellow teeth are revealed in an uncertain smile. 'Don't know.'

'Well, what about staying for the afternoon? Can't do any harm, can it?'

Healson, a master of coercion, leads Duff by the sleeve to a chair at one corner of the table. Duff sits down, looking seriously at the electronic jumble before him. Healson winks at me then leans over the table, explaining in oversimplified terms how to sort black, blue and red wires into neat straight strands. This irks me and I wonder if I've done the right thing in bringing Duff here. I feel a strange compulsion to go over to him, to snatch him away and take him back to wherever he wants to go. But I know I would only be making a fool of myself if I did. Rather I slip now from the room, hoping to rid myself quickly of my odd sense of guilt, of this anxiety like that of a father leaving his child at school for the first time, offering, as it seems, his own flesh and blood to the teeth of a system he cannot quite justify.

The rest of the day passes slowly as I attend to a new referral from the daughter of an old couple who believes her mother

[79]

is becoming mentally infirm and quite unable to look after her arthritic father. The house I'm let into is a bit squalid, but I can see little wrong with the woman, save for a little forgetfulness, and the daughter's fears are dismissed by the irascible old man as familial interfering, the first part of some horrific plan to get them both into a nursing home at the other side of town. I commiserate with them and agree to see the daughter again to try and dissuade her from her ill-considered ideas. Later, I'm back at the health centre, filling in for a sick colleague by interviewing a couple who are wanting to adopt a child, but I can do nothing save for a little prevarication and sympathy, and I send them away, knowing I have performed badly, that public concern over social service waffle would be completely vindicated in this case. I should have tried harder, but my mind's elsewhere and I'm thinking about Angela constantly, still scarcely able to believe in the idea of my having her with me, of sharing my life with someone else after all these years. The fact of it remains unapproachable, beyond analysis and facing in my mind. Rather I feel it as a presence, a robust, featureless mass inside me that might burst out at any minute, could be the divine understanding I seem to have been seeking lately. Or it may simply be a mistake, not yet made clear, that might end in humiliation for me, greater calamity for them. Though . . .

It's late into the night and the town is quiet and Angela's sleeping at my side. For myself there'll be little sleep, perhaps the last few hours before morning. I ease round again, turning slowly over on to my back so as not to disturb her. In the silvery wash of the streetlight I can see her slumbering, scowling face, her body making scarcely a ripple under the duvet, though she's hot, a little furnace inches away from me.

When I came home, hours ago, she was waiting to greet me, said she was glad I was back, that she had missed me. Laughing, I pointed out that she'd just moved in. 'S'that a problem?' she said. 'Ow long's it take to start carin' about someone?' She fussed around me the whole evening long, making my supper, telling me where I could find a clean shirt for the next day, saying her iron was far better than the old thing I used. She bewildered me all the while until she decided to go to bed, packing Sandy off too, saying I needed the last hour to myself – I was used to my own company and she'd not keep me from it all the time. I said it didn't matter, though I confess I needed the breathing space, a little time to realign myself with my own home, to adjust to the reallocation of space, time . . . emotions.

At midnight after a few reasserting, guiltily taken gins, I crept slowly up the stairs and undressed in the half-dark room, astonished at the familiarity of this ritual, how it might have been only the night before when I last slipped between the sheets to Caroline's side. And this night the warmth I knew then is just as intimate, seeming universal in its character and appeal, and I'm happy to have known it. To know it again, I'm thinking as Angela stirs, her face wretched with dream, calling 'Bob? Bob? Bob?' in a restive voice I can hardly recognize. I put my arm across her breasts, not sure how I am meant to comfort her. 'They were shoutin'. They were after me,' she sobs.

'Careful,' I whisper. 'Who was after you?'

'Gary an' his mob. It was awful. Friggin' 'orrible.'

'Only a dream. Can't harm you.'

I pull her close, her puppy sobs gentle against my bare chest. And it's a slight, sublime moment as I'm holding her (as I'm remembering now, my own tears aflow as I write) with her hand cupped over her face in quiet terror. 'Poor thing. Poor love,' I'm saying as I squeeze the soft bones of her fingers, kiss the salty lips. Someone needs me. She needs me. And I, a lifelong provider of succour, am here to help. Then she's smiling in the grey light and we melt into lovemaking. And the night passes quietly on, long, calm, grace itself.

'What is it?'

'A shirt, stupid.'

'I mean, what's it for?'

'I bought you it. Does there 'ave to be a reason? You're a funny bloke to please. Anyway, it's only off the market. Saw it when I was passin'. Thought you'd like it.'

I hold it up in front of me in the bar of the Black Dog. It has broad green and yellow stripes and an Australian Rules football motif across the front. 'A bit young for me?'

'Oh, go on. What yer like? You need brightenin' up a bit.'

'I'll put it on now. I'll do it in the gents'.'

'Not till I've ironed it, you won't,' Angela says, laughing, curling into herself like a reptile. 'D'you like it, then?'

I carefully fold the thing back into its plain brown bag, my stomach tightening. 'Can't remember the last time anyone bought me anything.'

'Give over. It's nowt. Nothing.'

'Oh, but it is, Angela. It's lovely. Beautiful,' I say, putting my arms around her.

'Now then, you two,' says the landlord, smiling from behind the bar. 'Bad enough with the kids. Don't forget Aids an' all. Can do without that in here.'

'You leave us alone,' says Angela. 'We're old enough. An' daft enough too, eh Bob?'

I say nothing, holding her hand, avoiding the patrician gaze of the landlord, this man an accessory now to Angela's and my

small society. This is the tenth time we have visited here. I have
counted them all.

Rycott breathes in the icy morning air with a single sharp
inspiration. He's wearing his double-breasted brown suit, a
flowery red tie, leather gloves. Suzie, huddled in a fake fur,
the tip of her nose crimson with the cold, stamps her feet and
yawns, watching the whining progress of a milk float as it pulls
away from the entrance to the tenement.

'Why so bloody early?' she asks.

'Best time,' says Rycott. 'Catch them unawares. And the
boy'll be able to see his new surroundings in daylight. Gives
him the chance to adapt.'

'What about the baby?'

'Get something on the lad, first. Then we'll be back for her.'

'You're having me on,' I say. 'We can't separate a mother
and baby.'

'No choice, I'm afraid. Sexual abuse of children, see. No
known limits to the depravity. We'd be failing in our duty.
You should know that, Robert.'

'Should I?' I say, though I cannot quite believe him, keeping
my arguments to myself, rapidly pondering how I might intervene later, perhaps by trying to find some way of separating
Brittan from Wakefield. But I'll not suggest it now, hardly the
time for it, alas.

'They're here,' says Rycott, stepping from the pavement to
wave an effeminate greeting to the police car as it slows to a
halt across the road.

'Shit. A panda. Uniforms too. You'd think they'd have a bit
of tact. They'll frighten the kid to death. Why's he dragged you
out on this anyway, Suzie?'

'Says it'll be good experience. Reckons I need it. Might be
running an operation like this myself before long.'

'Not if you can avoid it, you won't.'

'What do you mean?'

'Oh, never mind. The general wants his troops to the front.

Look,' I say, nodding towards Rycott who's beckoning and pointing at the door of the building, the two constables already making their way across the road. We follow, chasing through the door and up the staircase after them, Rycott and the two men already a flight ahead of us, their footsteps a tinny echo that rises to the top of the building.

When we reach the door of the flat we pause, all five of us breathing fast and deep, the two policemen – one older and heavily sideburned, his clean-shaven colleague looking no more than eighteen years of age – flanking Rycott. After a few seconds Rycott straightens up. 'Now?' he asks.

'Good a time as any,' the older man says, flatly.

Rycott thumps hard on the door and it's Wakefield who opens it, rubbing her eyes against the light from the landing window, sullenly roused by the presence of the officers. She tightens the belt of her dressing gown. 'Who're you lot?'

'Mrs Wakefield?'

'Might be.'

'My name is John Michael Rycott of Social Services and I have to inform you that we have reason to believe the welfare of your son, Thomas Wakefield, is being endangered. And under Section 28.2 of the Children and Young Persons Act 1969 I am empowered to remove him from this flat to a place of safety.'

'You what?'

'We've come for your lad, love,' says one of the officers. 'Let us in, eh?'

'My Tom? What're you talkin' about? No. No, you can't come in.'

But Rycott and the two policemen are already brushing past her and into the flat, with Suzie and I following. The woman looks at me hard. 'You? This your doin'?' But she doesn't wait for an answer, forcing her way past me in the narrow hall and through to the lounge where we all trail to find Brittan in pyjama bottoms and dressing gown, standing up from the table and his bowl of cereal.

'What the fuck?'

'Peter Brittan?' asks Rycott.

[85]

'So?'

'My name is John Rycott and I have to inform you that I am empowered by the Children's Act –'

'Children's Act? What bloody Children's Act? Worriz this?'

'– of 1969 to remove . . .'

'Where's the lad, Brittan?' asks the older policeman. 'Jack, check the bedrooms.'

The younger man nods and leaves the room.

'Ask them why they're doin' this. Tell them they can't have 'im,' Wakefield screeches at Brittan. 'Go on. Bloody say it.' Then she runs from the room, gathering the hem of her dressing gown up to her knees.

Brittan looks at me, pointing a shaking finger. 'It's you, innit? You're the one 'as done this.'

'I'm sorry, Mr Brittan.'

'You'll be sorry, pal.'

'Don't threaten, Brittan. There's a good chap,' says the officer.

'You can button it, an' all,' he says. 'There'll be plenty comin' your way when this is sorted out. Yer's stitched me up last time, but you won't this. Not if I can 'elp it. An' as for you, fat boy . . .' But he's interrupted by the return of the young policeman and the boy who is holding his hand.

Along the hall the boy's mother keens and wails. 'Yer can't. It's not bloody right.' Suzie goes to try and comfort her but Wakefield lashes out. 'Gerroff me, you bitch!' And she runs into a bedroom, slamming the door.

The boy, Tom, is wearing his school uniform, white-faced, cheeks quivering with incomprehension, an incipient fear that will spill over into tears at any moment. Brittan lunges forward, knocking over a dining chair, stooping and grabbing the boy's hands. 'Tell 'em, Tom. Tell 'em I'm all right. Been like a father to you, 'aven't I? Better'n your real dad. Say 'bout the fishin' an' that. An' that time we went to the fair. Remember the dragon rides? Tell 'em, Tom, eh? Don't let 'em do this to us.' But the boy shakes his head, pulling his hands loose and covering his face.

'Right. We'll go, shall we?' says Rycott with the only smile in the room.

Brittan straightens up, next to me now, close enough for me to feel the heat from his face, to smell the coffee on his breath.

'This what yer call doin' good, is it? This your idea of carin'?'

'It's our duty, Mr Brittan.'

'Well, yer've got it wrong. An' you'll be payin' for it. Don't you worry.'

The young officer, the boy, Rycott and Suzie begin filing out of the door, the older policeman waiting to guide me out of the room.

'You've a right to appeal,' I say, reluctant to leave, wishing I could explain myself, stop the pain we're causing, justify everything.

'Oh, I'll be appealin' all right.'

'I think we've done what we came to do,' the officer says to me, taking hold of my elbow. 'Away now, eh?'

'Scum,' says Brittan, eyes hard and glassy, drawing up the fear in me. 'Filthy, shitey scum,' he says, the words pulsing in my ears all the way out of the flat and down the staircase.

Back on the street the two policemen have returned to their car, the older one in the passenger seat, pencilling notes on a clipboard. He winds up his window to talk with his colleague. Suzie and the boy are on the back seat of Rycott's car, Suzie having said something to the lad which has made him smile effetely. Rycott is standing by the driver's door, taking off his gloves, looking pleased with himself.

'Now, Robert. I think it went well. Don't you?'

'I don't know. There's something wrong. I'm not so sure now. I'll know more when I've talked to the boy.'

His smile is crimped and knowing and he puts his arm round my shoulder.

'No need for you to trouble about that. You've performed well, my friend. Suzie and I'll take it from here.'

'It's my case, John.'

'So it is. And when we've got the result, the credit'll be all down to you. Mark my words,' he says, tapping my chest with his finger. 'God, but you're a worrier, Bob. You really are.' And he climbs into the car, starts it, and pulls away into the cold empty road.

The rest of the day finds me subdued, hardly able to concentrate on my dealings with people, ministering to their needs in a detached, dreamlike way, as if something has slipped out of gear inside me. It's not my way, I tell myself. But it's as if a fever has stolen into my system and is now building, sapping my usual ability to concentrate. Why didn't I insist on dealing with the boy? Am I losing my grip? Past caring? In the evening I am still in the same poor way.

'What's it like out there? Doin' what you do?'

'Bad, sometimes. Very bad.'

'Don't know 'ow yer do it. Not everyone could. I'd be 'opeless. People whingein' at me all the time,' Angela says, from her place on the rug in front of the electric fire. I watch her, noticing for the first time a little cluster of freckles on her bottom lip. And her nose has a slight kink and is upturned and bulbous at the end. I compare it with the daughter's which is straight and sharper. Then I look back at Angela, at her crossed bare ankles, the genteel way in which she holds a cigarette, fingers spread and dainty. And I'm wondering how much more I have yet to discover about her, how much more information her body will reveal to me in the future.

On the sofa Sandy is painting her toenails puce, occasionally pausing to look at the television, some film which is barely capturing the attention of any of us. Angela stirs from her position by my feet.

'So, you've 'ad a lousy day then,' she says, resting her chin on my knee, smiling.

'Not so hot.'

She squeezes my thighs, taking two fistfuls of skin.

'Maybe I could make it better for you.'

I feign a little distraction, as if still absorbed by my work problems, embarrassed, in truth, by Sandy's presence.

'I'll be OK. Don't worry.'

'Oh, but I do worry, Bob. Me an' Sandy, we worry all the time. Don't we, girl?'

Sandy appears to take no notice, turning to dabbing at her face with a ball of cotton wool soaked with pore cleanser.

'Anyway,' says Angela, winking hard, 'I'm away upstairs meself now. Been 'ard day for me too. Jeez, but I'm tired,' she says, stretching her arms high for effect.

When she has left the room Sandy begins filing her fingernails, pausing to squint at her hands between each furious rubbing action.

'Told you,' she says.

'Told me what?'

'That she'd be good for you,' she says, scratching an itch in her hair. 'She's 'appy. Better'n I've ever seen her.'

'That's all right, then, isn't it?' I say, feeling irritated by the girl's oblique remark.

'I love my mam.'

'Good.'

'I don't wanna see her hurt, neither.'

'And why should I want to hurt her?'

'It 'appens. Things are good. Then they go bad.'

'That right?'

She rests from all her activities, the litter of her bodily pampering scattered on the arms and cushions of my sofa.

'Why don't you go up? She'll be waitin'.'

I laugh emptily, blushing too.

'You're a strange kid, Sandra. How old are you, anyway?'

'S' that matter?'

'Yes, it does, as a matter of fact. We should be thinking about getting you into a school. You'll get me shot.'

'Fourteen, if you must know. And I'm already at school. The Friarage.'

'That's miles away.'

'So? I'll travel.'

I laugh again, competing with a rowdy lager advert on the television. 'I don't know . . .'

'Well? You goin' up to Mam or not?'

'When I'm ready, child.'

'Go. She's expectin' you. You're to make her happy. That's why we came 'ere.'

'What?'

'Just . . . you don't let her down.'

'I won't. Honestly,' I say, shaking my head.

'You better not,' she says, picking up the nail file again. 'I'm countin' on you. We both are. Think on.'

I like watching her at this time of day – the lumpy fur of her hair, the tiny shoulders beneath the threadbare towelling of her dressing gown. Her eyes are soft and brown. Not yet made up. Better without the warpaint. She lights a cigarette, blowing out the smoke which hangs in a cirrus above the untouched toast and marmalade I made for her.

'What yer lookin' at?'

'Nothing. Just you.'

She smiles, though it takes an effort.

'Another bloody day,' she says, her words mingled with a dry yawn.

'Oh? Something troubling you?'

'No. S'just . . . I don't know.'

I reach across the table and squeeze her wrist.

'You're not getting bored, are you? I'd hate the thought of that. Maybe you could do with a job. I could look out for something for you.'

'It's a thought, I suppose,' she says, squinting at the cigarette, flicking the filter with her thumb. 'We should be contributin' somethin' towards our keep.'

'No. That's not what I meant. I just thought . . .'

But then Sandy idles into the room in her nightdress, looking at her mother with a sleepy contempt.

'Yuk. D'you have to smoke in the mornings?'

Angela takes a hefty draw on the cigarette and stubs it out, half-finished, idly making grey circles with the butt in the ashtray. Then she smiles brightly at Sandy.

'So what's it today then, girl?'

'Don't know. Trip up town, p'raps?'

'Sounds good,' says Angela. And they begin chattering brightly, making plans for the shops they might visit. I make my way upstairs, leaving them to their warming conversation.

In the bedroom I stand half-dressed, trousers in my hand, looking at the pink havoc of the bedsheets where, not so long ago, Angela and I had lain. I stoop down and smell the linen for what warmth or fragrance of hers might still be there. Then I straighten up abruptly, alerted by their laughter from the room below with the odd feeling that they might have been watching me. I dress quickly, returning downstairs to offer a quick farewell. But something is holding me back, some quiet envy, perhaps, of the pleasure they take in making their companionship so exclusive.

'I've decided not to go in today,' I say, abruptly ending their chatter.

'Oh?' says Angela.

'Why shouldn't I take a day off now and then? Work hard enough, don't I?'

'Fine, then.'

'You gonna ring in sick?' asks Sandy, eyebrow raised, as if she believes me incapable of the deception.

'That's it. That's what I'll do. And then we could go out in the car somewhere. The three of us.'

'T'seaside!' Angela says. 'Buckets an' spades! Fish an' chips! Candy floss! The lot! God, 'aven't been there in ages.'

'Good idea. Why not?'

'Yeah, why not?' Sandy says soberly.

I made a weak excuse about a stomach bug to Rycott, though I have little talent for lying and he did not seem too convinced, saying the department had a heavy work load (when hadn't it?), hoping I would be better as soon as I could be. I had it

in mind to point out my near flawless sickness record, though
that would certainly have alerted him to my pretence. So I said
I hoped to be back the next day and insisted that all my own
cases should be set aside for me to catch up with personally on
my return. Then I went back upstairs and changed into the shirt
Angela bought me, self-consciously, madly hiding it beneath a
thick brown pullover at the last moment. Five minutes later we
left the house.

The drive to Bridlington takes an hour and a half. Angela's
sudden burst of enthusiasm for the idea seems to have given
way to a weak reflectiveness and she has said almost nothing
all the way here. Sandy, in the back, has read a magazine from
cover to cover looking up only to remark on the gathering
clouds and the possibility of a downpour. I say that would
be a good thing – it would empty the skies, clear the air – but
my comment inspires no optimism.

I leave the car in the harbour car-park and Angela and Sandy
trudge behind me, arm in arm, huddling against the wind
that blows straight and relentlessly from the brown, boiling
sea. As we walk along the harbourside I alternate my pace,
but they ape each gradation, seeming to want to maintain
the few yards' space between us. I continue on, choosing
the direction around the end of the harbour to the north
bay. Here some early season holiday-makers have gathered
among the few open rides of the fun-fair, the wind ripping
at the tarpaulin coverings of those not in use. At a waxworks
I stop and look at the posters and the ghoulish promises
they make about what's on show inside. Angela and Sandy
catch up with me, standing a few feet behind me. I turn to
face them.

'Fancy a look?'

Sandy screws up her nose and looks at her mother who
shakes her head.

'You go in,' says Angela. 'If you want.'

I should say no and make some joke about my being kept

[93]

for use in the exhibition if they found me wandering alone in there. But my temper's getting the better of me.

'Look, if you didn't want to come you need only have said. I took a day off work for this. Remember?'

'Take it easy,' says Angela. 'We're 'avin' a good time. S'nice.'

'Yeah. It's all right, Bob,' says Sandy.

Unmoved by their assertions I suggest that we make our way up into the town, away from the waterfront, where it might be warmer and we could find a café. They make the effort and agree, walking with more purpose, following me closely up the steps to the promenade and down a road of shops that leads into the town.

We pass half a dozen eating places, fish and chip shops, a pizzeria, a kebab house, dismissing each with a chilly playfulness, suggesting that not one of them is quite suited to our requirements which become more exclusive with every place we pass.

'Well,' says Angela. 'Seems there's just nowhere to eat in Brid.'

'Seems there's nothing much,' I say. 'Ah well.'

'I'm not so hungry anyway,' says Angela.

'Not me, an' all,' says Sandy, still clutching her mother's arm.

'Home, then?' I suggest.

'In a bit,' says Angela. 'We'll just walk for now, eh? S'nice bein' somewhere else. Makes a change.'

So we walk on away from the busier streets, over a railway crossing towards the older part of the town, a sea fret rolling over the houses and gathering along the roads like folds of cold steam. And we're saying nothing to each other, though their disgruntlement of an hour before seems to have disappeared altogether. Then we see it, set back from the road, its walls painted summer green with yellow crenellations around the roof – bright, frivolously coloured architecture that you do not see back home. And there's a garden with a pebble drive and ivy trailing in ragged crescents along the fence. Sea Croft. A guest house. For sale.

'God, I could live there,' says Angela. 'It'd be like bein' on holiday all the time. Imagine.'

'Pretty, isn't it?' I say.

We move a few steps further along the moist pavement, still quite spellbound by the place. Angela begins chattering hurriedly about how her father used to bring her and her mother to Bridlington when they were kids. But it was always only for the day. They couldn't afford to stay anywhere, not a single bloody night, never mind a whole week. She wonders what life might really be like here, having it in mind, she says, to play the sequin-gowned, mule-slippered hostess, with big ear-rings dangling in the hair she'd grow gypsy-fashion. 'Like ah-so!' she says, bunching the thick locks to one side of her head, drawing her denim jacket tight about her waist, standing tiptoe in a way that arouses me, prompts a tickling tumescence ... Then Sandy joins in the fantasy, saying that I could run the bar while she supervised the cleaners we'd have – at the lowest rates, because we'd want the profits for ourselves – to keep the drudgery from our lives. I can contribute nothing, can only listen to their mounting elaborations until, a moment before they reach the silly point when they are about to start dancing on the pavement, I intervene, suggesting we take a look round the place.

Sandy pushes her hands into the pockets of her coat, looking pointedly at her mother. Angela is statuesque, her eyes momentarily downcast, then suddenly wide in the smudges of her mascara. 'Oooh? D'yer think we dare?'

'What's there to dare?' I say.

And fifteen minutes later, after I've rung the agent from a call box, we're being shown round by the owner, an old man called Baxter whose wife has died and who's looking to retire from the guest house game. 'No point now,' he says. I tell him I understand, keeping a careful eye on Angela whose unstoppable fantasies have now become detached, wistful dreams as she explores the big kitchen, treads carefully on the soft carpet in the sprawling lounge. When we are left alone to explore the empty rooms upstairs, she looks at me with a tired, resigned expression.

'Better be off now, eh?' she says.

'What's the hurry? Haven't seen the garden yet.'

'Oh, come on, Bob. Stop wastin' the fella's time. We could no more afford this place than bleedin' fly.'

'I could.'

'What?'

'The asking price isn't so high. If I could knock him down a bit, get rid of my own place.'

'You're not bein' serious?'

'Aren't I?'

'But . . . your job, an' that?'

'What about it?'

An hour later and we're sitting in a pub I've deliberately chosen, overlooking the harbour. On the table in front of me are pages torn from my diary, scattered like playing cards, each covered in pencilled figures, evidence I have brought before the two of them that I could afford the place, at a pinch, and that we could make it work together. Sandy could forget about school for good, I suggest. No one would be any the wiser. But while her mother goes to the bar, delirious with fresh possibilities, the daughter is cool, making little spreading arcs in a pool of spilt lager with her fingernail.

'You'll break 'er heart,' she says.

'What do you mean?'

'It'll never come off.'

'Oh? And why not?'

''Cos she won't leave that town. She's its property. We both are.'

'That's rubbish. Stop spoiling it,' I say, angrily. 'Your mother's as keen as I am. She deserves a chance like this. We all do.'

'An' another thing. There's your job. Yer'll not leave it. You can't. It's part of you. Yer've been doin' it too long.'

'If you're saying I'm too old . . .'

But Angela is back at the table with drinks and a huge packet of crisps for Sandy.

'Now then, you two. What's the big secret?'

'Nothing,' I say. 'There's no secret. Is there, Sandra?'

But the girl just inhales softly, folding her arms, looking out of the window at a coble swaying perilously out of the harbour mouth.

On the way home Angela rests her head on my shoulder, listening contentedly while I, in defiance of the sullen daughter sitting behind us, fuel the day's dream with estimations of the bookings we might get, using the hard reality of figures – annual gross profits, overheads, the amounts we would have to set aside for income tax – to bewitch the mother and silence the girl. And by the time we have reached my house, deep into the night, it is as if the decision has been made, the plans worked out months, years ago. Sandy goes up to her room without a word. But, in the kitchen, Angela thoughtfully waylays me and we make vigorous love to seal the pact of our making a new life together.

For the next two days my duties were completely subordinate to the consuming secret I suddenly possessed – the possibility of starting life all over again. I nurtured the desire, allowing it to develop with each new detail, each delicious problem I could think of, analyse and conquer. I made genuine calculations about how I might be able to afford Sea Croft (a name to which I became more attached than my own), deciding that to get the loan I needed I would probably have to lie and say I still intended to be employed in some capacity as a social worker while running the business. I made an agenda for when it might all begin to happen, a date at the end of the week for putting my house up for sale, a tentative deadline for tendering my resignation. And I watched the money I spent, making trifling economies in the buying of lunch, dispensing with a daily newspaper, as if each tiny saving could convert another fragment of the dream into a truth, reality, the shared future I'd never once considered could be for me.

In the evenings, when Sandy was out of the way, I would mention it to Angela, keeping the more elaborate details to myself, summarizing the whole strategy in no more than half a dozen sentences.

'Property market's a bit flat at the moment. But that suits us as much as it does Baxter,' I'd say suddenly. 'Interest rates are favourable just now and the forecast's even better,' I'd add, enthusiastically imbuing my talk with the jargon of the business world I imagined myself entering.

'I'm better leavin' it to you,' Angela would reply, putting her arm around me, drawing me closer to her on the sofa we claimed for ourselves once Sandy had gone up to bed.

'Wish I'd saved more, now. Could have done. But, well, you never think something like this will ever happen.'

And that would be an end to it. I wanted to talk about it so much that I could hardly bring myself to mention it, capable only of these random references, satisfied, glad that I must do all the work myself and that one day, soon as could be, it would be coming off.

On the Thursday I have made an appointment with the manager of my bank and I'm hanging around the health centre, putting off all telephone callers, in such a state of tension that I can fake no semblance of the social worker's industriousness. I'm pacing the carpeted floor between my desk and the window, calculating what credentials I might have with the bank. I never overdraw, which must count for something. But the few hundred pounds I have in a building society account will not say much about me. I'll not even mention the paltry amount I have in premium bonds. Then for half an hour I try to rehearse my approach in the interview.

The man I'm to see is called Goodhugh. Just his name. That's all I know about him. I picture him as young, slim, clean-shaven, quiet-mannered, and I wonder how sympathetic he might be to the social worker's lot in this world, imagining all kinds of pleas and grouses, stored up in these last sixteen years, that I might put to him by way of explaining my motives for wanting to go into business. Though how much of the human element might count in situations like this? All of it? Any of it? Probably nothing. Best stay off that tack. Sentiment won't be worth a ha'penny to a bank manager. Might make things worse, if it looks as if my heart is ruling my head. A sudden small despair leads me to slump in my seat behind the desk. I should have drawn up some kind of business forecast, a projected trading balance, or whatever they call it. And it should have been typed, in a neat folder. Oh God, oh dear, how little I know of these things. But there is a last resort, at the moment before I see myself falling to my knees in a room on the top floor of Barclay's Bank in Market Street. There's my brother, Matthew, I'll say. He's a wealthy man. Probably more than willing to secure the loan. I'll say we've discussed the matter – though I haven't seen him in a long time and I don't know how I'd ever be able to ask such a favour.

The permutations carry on, exhaustingly, prompting Malcolm, who today seems annoyingly unable to leave the office without me, to remark on my preoccupations.

'Things on my mind, mate,' I say dismissively. 'You know how it is.'

'Anything I c-can help with?'

'No. It's nothing.'

'I-I'd be only too p-pleased to help you, R-Robert.'

'I know. You've said it before. And I'm grateful, Malcolm. I really am. But this is nothing. A small matter. Don't worry about it.'

Then, forty minutes before I am due to be in the bank manager's office, Rycott puts his head round the door, startling Malcolm to his feet.

'You going to be here all day, Malcolm?'

'J-j-just going, Mmm-Mr Rycott.'

'Robert, a word, please,' Rycott says, beckoning me out of the office.

In the corridor he wipes a minute sliver of spittle from his lips, and leans elegantly against the wall, close to me.

'Bit of a problem, Bob.'

'Problem? With what? The Wakefield kid?'

'No. That's all right. Coming along swimmingly. In fact, we're hoping for a result any day now.'

'You mean you still haven't got a statement from him?'

'As such, no. But it won't be long now.'

Malcolm comes out of the office, brushing past us with his briefcase clamped high and hard against his breast, skittering through the doctor's waiting room, bumping into a young woman, spluttering excessive apologies before he makes it out of the far door.

'No,' says Rycott. 'It's that Maisie Bertowski woman.'

'Oh no. Not her again. I thought that was all worked out. The GP said there was nothing wrong with her.'

'Not such a hot diagnosis, I'm afraid. She's holed up in her house. Keeps opening the lavvy window, chucking pots and pans at people in the street. Police are there now.'

'Give me a break, eh, John? Can't Malcolm go?'

'I need you, Robert.'

'What about Suzie, then? It'd be much better with a woman.'

'She's not got the experience. Besides, I want her in my office today. Taking the calls,' he says, looking along the corridor as if awaiting an unwanted visitor. 'Listen, Bob. This one's down to you. I'm counting on you. I know you won't let me down. There's a good chap.'

'Again?' I say.

'What?'

'Every blessed dirty job in the book, John.'

'Come on, Robert. Work to do. Good to be ministered, eh?' he says, evading the small confrontation I have in mind. He taps me on the lapel with his knuckle, smiles, then is away before I can say another word.

So I drive across the town at a murderous speed, arriving to find two constables leaning against their car, their sleepy faces turned up into the sunshine. A policewoman is standing in the ragged garden next to the front door. I get out of the car, march into the garden while, for my benefit, I presume, she raps on the door, shouts through the letterbox, stands back and peers up at the curtained bedroom windows.

'You see? Nothing,' she says.

I'm summoned round to the rear of the house by the two constables to witness one of them breaking open the back door with one efficient blow of a hefty axe. The door swings open impressively and the other constable gestures towards the interior.

'You trying first?' he asks.

'I think that's why I'm here,' I say.

Inside, the fusty smell of old Maisie assaults me, strikes me as affronting. In the kitchen is the ancient cooker, its lines obscured by caked, burned food. In the next room furniture and cardboard boxes have been piled high to block the light from the window and the damp flock wallpaper curls down from the picture rail. Behind the front door in the hall I see a spill of unopened mail and in the tiny lounge to my left I find the carcass of a small skeletal white dog I cannot remember from my last visit. It draws the attention of a few drunkenly circling flies.

Wildly conscious of the passing of time, I close the door on the room and quickly make my way upstairs where, in the brown light of the shaded bedroom, standing beside a piss-soaked mattress on the floor, I find Maisie.

She's wearing at least three dresses, three cardigans, and a flowery headscarf knotted bulkily around her neck – clothes which serve to disguise her slightness, to give her a sadly comical look. In her hand is a ragged old pomander which she's trying to tuck up in her skirts, for some reason. She wedges it beneath her arm, then brings it out again, looking at it quizzically as if it's just appeared on her flesh, magically, for the first time. Then she senses my presence, stares at me, the sweating fat man, a stranger in her bedroom.

'So you've come, then,' she says, as if she's been expecting me all along.

'Looks like it.' I attempt a smile. 'Shall we go out now?'

'Oh, I'll not be troubled to do that. I'm all right where I am, thank you very much,' she says, her attention now drawn by a chink in the curtains.

'Come on, Maisie. Out now. There's a girl, eh?'

'No. I'll stay here. If you don't mind.'

'But I do mind, Maisie. Really I do,' I say, taking a step forward. 'I haven't the time for hanging about here all day.'

[103]

'That's your worry then, isn't it?' she says, though I see her hands trembling a little as she reaches to pull at the corner of the curtain.

I look at my watch, then push my tight fists into my jacket pockets. I've done this a thousand times, usually quite prepared to sit it out, reasoning with the unreasonable, the deranged, the dissolute, all day, if need be, until I've worn them down, made them make the move themselves to wherever it is I want them to go. But today . . . I search in my memory for all that I can remember about Maisie, devising a plot more despicable than the mere threat of my intimidating physical presence. I know she had a daughter, dead for many years.

'Remember Jo, Maisie?'

'Jo?'

'That's right girl,' I say, with a pernicious gentility. 'Your daughter, Jo.'

'What about her?' she says, the old eyes constricting to pinpricks.

'Well, she's come to see you, Maisie. She's outside. In the yard. Wouldn't you like to see her? Been a long time, hasn't it? You do remember Jo, don't you?'

'Course I remember her. She's my bairn.'

'So how's about coming down to see her?'

She looks puzzled at first, then she wrings her hands, smiling wanly.

'I shall have to do something with my hair first.'

'You're hair's fine, Maisie. Looks wonderful,' I say, edging another half-pace closer, reaching out my hand. 'Come on. Good girl. She might be gone if we're not quick.'

She ignores my hand, shuffling softly past me to the top of the stairs, her thin smile fading to a thanatophile parting of the grey lips. I follow her, feeling both triumphant and a little sickened with myself, jollying her down each worrying step until, after what seems an age, we are at the bottom. Then she sniffs the cooler fresh air, sees the open back door and turns quickly. But only to find my large frame blocking her path.

'Let me past,' she says. 'It's a trick. I'm not going out there.'

[104]

'But you have to, Maisie,' I say, with no more energy for pretence. 'Come on. You can't stay here.'

I put my arms around her, laughing for the sake of any police officer who might be able to hear us. She stamps at the floor, tries to bite my hands. And I begin to crush her, far harder than is necessary, lifting her off her feet, swinging her from the hall to the back room, the smell of her, the crackling of her bones, her gargling protests repulsing me in a way that I've never been bothered before. Then she manages a back kick with her heel that stings my shin. I drop her angrily, but she falls with the surefootedness of a cat, turning and hissing grotesquely, risibly.

'Animal,' she says. 'I know who you are now. Beast. Bugger. Animal that you are.'

She closes her eyes, looking about to faint, before she gets a grip on herself, tearfully marching out of the room and through the back door. I follow, rubbing at the warming wound on my leg.

'Trouble?' asks one of the officers.

'A bit,' I say, leaning against the splinters of the door frame, sweating, trying to conceal the inexplicable trembling that's come over me. 'You're a tough one, Maisie. I'll give you that.'

'Pig,' she says, trying to spit at me, the dribble only running down her chin. 'Fat bloody pig,' she adds, tearfully taking the offered arm of the policewoman who walks her away to the waiting car.

'You coming with us?' asks the officer.

'Can't. Another case. Very urgent. Tell them at the hospital I'll be along soon as I can. They'll understand,' I say, hobbling back round the house towards my own car, leaving the man standing in the road, watching me with no faint hint of suspicion in his look.

I'm nearly an hour late, but Mr Goodhugh understands. He's about twenty-one years old, slim, scrupulously shaven, mild-mannered. But he's a fine man, Mr Goodhugh. A saint.

[105]

A thinker, too. Says he's always fancied social work himself. Reckons it'd be real work. Necessary. Not like being in a bank, shuffling bits of paper round all day. What's money? What's so important about it? He looks out of his office window at the town. The things that go on down there, he says, with a shake of the neatly groomed head. He doesn't know the half of it. Doesn't know any of it, he says. There are people out there needing help. The homeless. The abused. The mad. And the bad. A loan? No problem. Not for the likes of you, Mr Munro. Good risks, social workers. Besides, everyone's feeling bullish about the English seaside trade, these days. And, by the way, if he really decides to go in for social work, would I put in a good word for him? Delighted. Proud to, I say, shaking the limp white hand, making my way out to the street, feeling like singing for the first time in my life.

The exertions of the day have left me feeling as if I've been washed up on a beach, exhausted, but a survivor, and a delicious sense of calm overrides all my earlier, frantic mental activities. I drive steadily away from the town centre, both excited and a little frightened by this rapid development in my plans. But there's to be no looking back now, the design is filling out of its own accord, taking shape, and I'm more than prepared to follow its progress. Now I shall have to get the house valued and up for sale and approach Baxter's agent, perhaps the old man himself, with a firm offer, a solid and actual figure that now lends a certain sobriety to the affair.

The thought of returning to the health centre is more unappealing than ever before, though I have it in mind to show myself before the day is out, to force myself somehow to address the pile of messages and referrals, the agenda I have abandoned today. A new and applied sense of caution replaces the headiness of a few minutes before – I shall have to be fair with Rycott, since, if nothing else, I shall need my last salary to help fund some part of the exercise. But today I can spare one more hour to go home and give Angela the news before I return to work and confront him.

I drive into my street, looking at the dull old place anew, feeling a pang of nostalgia as if I have already left these proud little houses, as if their history is already continuing without knowledge of me. I find a parking space thirty yards from my front door and leave the car unlocked, nodding to a neighbour, a fat ageing woman who passes on her way, arms pulled at the side by two heavy shopping baskets. And it strikes me as sad that after all this time, there is no one down here to whom I will be obliged to say goodbye. How little effort I made to try and get to know people here. I shall have to work harder with the guest house, learn a little subservience, a few social graces, nothing excessive, just enough to please the boarders. This thought imparts a shiver of excitement in the pit of my stomach as I open my door, a sense of icy apprehension that still does not dissipate as I stare unbelievingly at the spoil of stuffed bags and suitcases that fills the tiny hall from end to end.

Sandy appears from the lounge, wearing a tartan cape I've never seen before. She plumps herself on the biggest suitcase, sucking her thumb.

'Hello, Uncle Bob.'

'What's all this? What's going on?'

'Thingth have changed. D'yer thee, Uncle Bob?'

'Why're you talking like that? What're you up to?'

'It'th thimple, Uncle Bob.'

'Stop it. Stop calling me that.'

'I thed to Mam, what're we gonna do if we move out of here? She thed we'd go to a new friend she'th found and Bob'th yer uncle.'

She effects a chilling girlish laugh which makes me want to hit her.

'Little witch. Where's your mother?'

'Upstairs,' she says, drily, taken aback, perhaps, by my angry proximity to her in this small cramped space. 'She'll not be pleased to see you. You weren't expected back till later.'

'I can see that,' I say, pushing past her, stumbling over the bags and up the stairs.

In the bedroom I find her, wearing a red satin jacket, white trousers and white tassled boots. The warpaint's there too, in thick black arrowheads around the eyes, and the air is sickly with her scent. On the bed is a blue canvas holdall she's filling with what appears to be the last of her clothes. She knows I

am here, but it doesn't stop her. I stand inside the doorway,
feeling heavy and faint.

'Angela?'

''Ullo, Bob,' she says, matter-of-factly. 'You weren't meant to
be back at this time.'

'So I see.'

She scoops a bundle of rolled-up tights from the shelf in the
wardrobe and drops them in the bag, returning for a handful
of pastel-coloured pants.

'Am I getting an explanation, then?' I ask.

'Don't see as there's much to explain.'

'How can you say that, Angela? Tell me. Say what's wrong.'

She pauses, standing stiff and unsure of herself, the whites
of her eyes showing in the bed of mascara as she looks to her
side, towards me.

'S'over Bob. I'm sorry. It's finished.'

'What's finished? What are you doing to me? We've got
plans. Remember? Christ, Angela. Bridlington. Sea Croft. What
are you doing to us?'

I'm smiling, but the tears are welling. I squeeze them back,
knowing how she could despise such emotion in a man. Then
I see it, the letter on the crumpled pillow of our unmade bed.
I pretend to have noticed nothing, taking a few steps to my
side before I lunge for it. But she's spotted my fat clumsy
move and, nimble as a sprite, she snatches it up. A brief,
farcical tussle begins as I reach for the thing and she whips
under my flapping arms, rolling neatly over to the other side
of the bed and on to her feet. She rams the letter into the
pocket of her trousers while I'm stumbling, floundering on
the bed like a seal. I lash out at her, grabbing only air, easily,
characteristically the loser in this our first ever fight. I sit up
on the bed, smiling still, for the way it conceals the horror
inside me.

'Let me have it.'

'No.'

'Well at least tell me what you've put in the fucking thing.'

'S' nothing. Just, you know, sorry an' that,' she says, busying herself again with her packing, trying to hide some breathlessness of her own.

I begin laughing then, cold, unearthly laughter that visibly upsets her.

'I don't believe you. I'm offering you a new life. Something you've always dreamed of, you said. A chance. And you're throwing it in my face.'

'I'm sorry.'

'Stop saying that. I'm sick to death of sorry.'

'Ah . . . I just can't face it. I live here. In this town. It's me. Where I'm from. Allus been from.'

She clatters her make-up things from the dressing table to a flowery soap bag, tossing it unfastened into the holdall where its contents tip out again among her clothes.

'It's her, isn't it? She's put you up to this.'

'I just want to say I'm grateful, Bob. You got us out of a fix an' I'll always be glad of that.'

'What's she been saying to you?' I say, shuffling to the side of the bed.

'An' you've done all right out of me, too. You'll not disagree with that.'

'What's she said?'

'It's been good. Fun.'

'What did she say to make you want to do this, Angela?'

'Nowt. Nothing,' she says, a wince of anguish pinching her features. 'It's my decision. I think it's for the best. We're off now.'

'Who's this friend, then?'

'S' nobody. Just someone as'll put us up for a bit.'

'Not Gary? Don't tell me you're going back to him?'

She's crying herself now, little convulsions that make her shoulders bob and sway. Then Sandy's calling from the foot of the stairs.

'Taxi's here, Mam. Look sharp!'

I cannot help myself, standing and taking hold of her, squeezing her till there cannot be an atom of breath left in her small, sweet body.

[111]

'Please, Bob . . .'

'Ange. Angela? Not this?'

'Ma-am?' comes the hated voice again.

'Let go, Robert. Yer hurtin'.'

She wriggles herself loose, banging my nose with her head. Then it's as if time is slowed to a standstill as I watch her, the asinine smile still on my face, still there as she picks up the bag with one elegant arcing stoop, as she skips in apparent slow motion from the room. And I'm powerless to stop her, knowing all the calamity that these few moments will bring for me, thinking, You're a good girl, Angela. It's me that's at fault. Me that's bad. All bad. And still I'm grinning like the fool I am, have always been, as I hear her clumping down the stairs, exchanging some low angry words with her daughter. The taxi pips its horn outside and there's a rustling and herding of the bags through the door and the cheery maddening voice of the driver come to help with the load. And there's still time, aeons of it, to go down there and intervene, to stop this madness. Still time, a lifetime yet before the front door is slammed, twice for effect, and I am left alone in the quiet bedroom in the empty house, from where I do not stir for many hours.

So I spend the night alone with the silence of the house, feeling myself entering into, becoming part of this silence, my own body being no more than a distant ghostly notion. The light fades by subtle degrees, shading the room, making new fragmentary contours – floating edges of furniture, soft and sinister shadows – until at last I make the conscious effort to stir myself. It's late, late in the night when I make my way to the bathroom and urinate for an interminable length of time. Then the words begin appearing in my mind like dark desert flowers – Ingratitude. Blame. Bad. Dead end. Over – and other, random selections from the language of the town, in the voice of some unknown, commiserating man of the streets – Bad news, eh, pal? Tough shit. Rough, that – it says. I should do something, I say to myself. Put the light on at least. But I can't face it. I undress and get into the bed, though there's no sleep, no dreams to offer relief, just the silence and a clutching of the sheets in my hands, the bed already musty with only my own presence. Pointless. Waste. In the shite. Can't trust 'em, you know. Give 'em an inch and they'll take a hundred friggin' miles, says the voice, beginning again, stopping only when I've pleaded, shouted into my pillow that it must leave me alone.

It's nine the next day when I make myself get up, forcing myself to perform the rituals of shaving, washing, dressing. I put on my best suit for no particular reason. It feels, yes, tight, nipping under the arms, the waistband of the trousers digging between two soft tyres in my stomach. And there's a pulsing ache in my right temple that I cannot massage away. I'm ready to go now, but the minutes pass and I do not move, superficially concerned about my appearance. I should look in the mirror. Yet who will I see there but good old Bob? Someone everybody trusts. Steady. Reliable. Bit crusty. But a good sort. A saint, really. Then the voice in my head is my own, and it's saying just one thing, over and over: There'll be no weeping.

When, at last, I make it to the health centre, a full two hours late, it's to find Malcolm pacing up and down, imbecilically catching his thigh on the corner of his own desk with every turn of the floor.

'Go on, then,' I say, surprised by the evenness of my voice, setting my coat down on the filing cabinet, though this last small action seems to have been performed by someone else. Again, someone I do not know.

'Aw sh-shit, Robert. Y-you should have been here.'

'Why?' I say, yawning.

'R-Rycott.'

'Now what? You in bother again?'

'S-s-not me, R-Robert. N-not, oh f-fuck, not this time.'

'So?'

'It's y-you he's after.'

'Really? Now that does interest me,' I say, avoiding my seat, old Bob's chair, opting to prop myself against the lip of the desk.

'Th-that kid you had b-brought in. C-can't get a s-statement from him. G-good as admitted he was l-lying, t-trying it on with us. The mother s-says he's done it before. Gets j-jealous of her boyfriends. And the m-man's g-got this appeal coming up. L-looks like being s-successful too. Apparently he'd been f-fitted up. S-same situation as this. Down s-south somewhere.'

'Oh?'

'And then th-there's that l-lad you got a job for.'

'Duff?'

'S-s-him. Hasn't been t-turning up to work.'

'Hardly a hanging offence.'

'But s-stuff's been going missing f-from the workshop. Two and t-two and all that. They've c-complained about him. R-Rycott w-wants to know what you were d-doing getting him in there in the f-first place. S-says you'd no business.'

'That a fact?'

'And there's m-more. The B-Bertowski woman. Arrived at the hospital c-covered in bruises. She's s-saying you did it. S-seems she's not s-so daft as we thought. R-Rycott'll be back in an hour. G-gone up to try and s-smooth it over with the big ch-cheeses at District. S-see, they're involved too, now. We're all in it. Up-up to our f-fucking necks. Aw Ch-Christ, Bob. What're we going to d-do?' he's saying, lips wet with saliva, leaning exhausted on his desk.

Outside the window the morning breeze is playing with the small white clouds, tugging them into each other, drawing them down to the earth. In the waiting room next door there's an argument between the duty doctor and a shrill disconsolate woman. On my desk the notes, referrals and memos cover its entire surface. And the phone is ringing, for the fifty-thousandth time, someone wanting me, trying to send some message for me to deliver them from whatever hell it is they've got themselves into today.

'Nothing.'

'Wh-what?'

'Just that,' I say, taking a single step to the filing cabinet. 'I'm going. Off. No more. Can't take any more. Had enough.'

'B-be reasonable, R-Robert.'

'I am being reasonable,' I say, picking up my coat. 'It's the best thing for all of us. Goodbye, Malcolm.'

'R-Robert!' he yells.

But I'm away now, through the waiting room and the doctor's cooling argument, out of the main doors and to my car in ten huge strides and five seconds flat.

I drive out of the car-park, looking at the centre with a rarefied appreciation, at the wall and the blue entrance sign that seem more familiar than ever, as if alive, as if each brick and piece of wood and gram of tarmac knew, on my arrival just ten minutes ago, that I should soon be out here again, making this journey, embarking on this day when I'm to throw it all away. It's as if the earth and sky and wind and cloud have been unified into a single heartbeating creature and I'm alone in its mind, known there, having been waited for. It's right, this. The right thing to do. I have acted well, impulsively, the only way to act, to feel something truly. And now it's done and the relief is exhilarating, goes to the core. Don't know where I'm going now, but it doesn't matter. Nothing has ever mattered, if I had but realized it. Nothing so important as a fart in a hurricane.

I stop at a red light in an old suburb, feeling more relaxed than I've felt in my whole forty-three years. I look around me, wishing, perhaps, to see someone else in the same madcap frame of mind, some means of reflecting, recognizing this release. But it's all inside me, no one among the women clustering round the grubby little shops, the shoal of men on their bikes making their way home from the dawn shift at the liquorice factory, knows about this, will ever know this overwhelming sense of sanity. Half-lives all. Made that way. Had them designed for them by the centuries that went before. And they're glad of it, relieved, I'm sure, if they do but know it, that they do not have to think as I do, that they need not think at all. Best that way. Comfortable. Oh, but if I could only share this wisdom with someone, have an audience to whom I could impart my sudden unravelling of the great secrets of life. Then, as the red light blinks to amber, I see a shape I know – rounded shoulders, greasy blond hair swinging and lurching. Without a thought I reach over and open the passenger door, shouting at him to get in. He looks over a bare grass verge, seeing me, having no time to think, perhaps drawn by the wild look that must be in my eyes. He scrambles into the car. The driver of the pick-up behind me sounds his horn and speeds past, red-necked with anger. I laugh. Duff laughs too, as I force the car into the snarl of traffic I have caused myself.

'No work today, Billy boy?'

'Couldn't be arsed.'

And we are both in instantly, reciprocally good spirits, brilliantly dispelling the absurd pretences with which we have entertained each other over the last few weeks. I'd swear too, that he knows exactly what's been going on this morning.

'Where we off, then?' he asks, settling down into his seat.

'Anywhere. Right?'

'Yeah.'

So, I'm driving out of town at eighty miles an hour, the engine of my old banger giving out a new fulsome drone as if it too wants to be involved in the adventure, an agent to the spontaneous burst of release that's inspiring me. I watch only the road, the little black cakes of birds flattened on the tarmac, the houses an apocryphal blur in my peripheral vision, soon giving way to the first green mounds of the moors, the flying yellow fields of rape, and the sensuous undulations of the motorway. I reach ninety-five, ninety-eight, before I slow a little, my foot aching on the accelerator. I glance at Duff who seems quietly disappointed by this, so I switch on the radio and we are instantly treated to a joke from an avant-garde American comedian who says he's had this nightmare about being chased out of his house by a giant spider – with the head of a social worker. We both laugh loud and heartily, me thumping the steering wheel in appreciation. But then I'm feeling bored, and seeing a dirt track ahead I pull over, letting the car bump and lurch along until the way seems impassable and the engine wants no more of the excursion. I turn off the radio and let my aching wrists drop into my lap, looking with a rare serenity at the folds of the distant hills, purple and raised like the backs of sleeping animals.

'A walk, now, I think.'

But beside me Duff's lips are gathered in a dismissive curl, an ugly indifference. 'Nah.'

'Please yourself,' I say, and I get out, stumbling on the unexpected incline on which the car has come to rest, slamming the door harder than I had intended.

The air is soft and silky, soothing on my face, as I make my way over the yielding tufted pasture to the silvery crags that draw me. Two minutes later and I'm scrambling up the scree towards a gap in the first rocks through which I shall be able to get to the other side, out of sight of Duff. I pause to look back, seeing him getting slowly out of the car, looking about him, back to the motorway and the monotonous swish of its traffic. Then he's turning, looking at the path I have made among the ferns, taking the first tentative steps in my direction.

But this would-be assassin, when he's made it round the crag, finds no laughing madman, his flabby chest bared for the knife the boy might be carrying, no burnt-out altruist poised above a moorland abyss, inviting him to apply the final, lightest of pressure to fulfil both their wishes (would that he had – the dream scenario, I'm thinking now). No, all he finds is a crumpled fool in his best suit, sitting beneath the ravens that swoop from the rocks above, blown by the winds that trouble the gorse and dab at the shingle at his feet. And he's weeping.

Nothing to do, says the unknown voice, here again as I drive back to the town. Duff seemed to disregard my fit of tears completely, amusing himself by pitching stones off the hillside with only the tiniest of smiles to show that he had thought anything at all about my behaviour. And for him, I now have the same indifference. The game's up, says the voice as I drop Duff off at the Albert Hall Hotel, watching him scoot away to the steps without offering me a word of farewell. 'It's over,' I say aloud.

I drive a little further on and park in a side street. I cannot face the prospect of going home – there's nothing there for me now. But where? Where can I go? The only other place I have ever really known in this town, where I could be admitted unchallenged, is the health centre. But that's closed to me now. For ever. A thought that suffuses me with some grim strength. I get out of the car and walk, unsteadily, to the end of the street and round the corner. There I see the Black Dog, its lights bright against the orange twilight. My arrival here is quite unintentional, seeming the result of some awful conspiracy of fate. Without a further thought, neither needing nor wanting to, I cross the empty road and enter the open bar door.

The landlord, seeming to be asleep on his feet, opens his eyes at my arrival. But he does not recognize me without Angela. He's a part of the past now, I'm thinking, party to Angela's leaving me, ranking on her side.

'Drink, please.'

'Right place for it,' he says. ''Appen you could give me a clue as to what drink you're after?'

'Scotch. Large one.'

He brings the drink from the lounge bar and I light a cigarette, alarmed to see my hand shaking. There's no one else in the room save for an amazonian woman, swathed in a long blue coat, sitting alone by the fruit machine.

'Big girl, that.' A stupidly contrived aspersion, aimed at ingratiating myself with the man.

He snorts, brings my change. 'An' you'll not be hidin' behind a sapling yourself, will you?'

'That's right,' I say, loudly, masking the pains I feel from his affront, from my own hopeless efforts at small talk. I drain the whisky and feel its heat instantly in my empty stomach. 'Another.'

As he goes to refill the glass a group of five young men enter the room and gather about the bar to my left. I light another cigarette from the butt of the first, sipping more slowly now, already aware of that first, refined stage of intoxication, a lightness in the veins. And I want more of it, to chase it the way drinkers do. When the men have been served I ask for a triple, down it, and ask for another, slurring my words.

'Got a thirst on there?' says one of the men, all of whom look at me in turn.

'S'right, mate. Bad day. Fucking bad day,' I say, for some reason seeming to have adopted the persona of the voice that has been whispering in my thoughts.

'No answer, that,' says another. 'Screw yer liver up, drinkin' like that.'

'Oh? And how'd you know? When's the likes of you ever worry about me, eh?' I say.

'Sorry for breathin',' says the man, turning into the group.

'Nah. No. Listen,' I'm saying, easy now with the drink and the identity I have assumed. 'D'you know what I do for a living, eh? Any idea?'

'Brain surgeon,' says one.

'I know,' says another, a short ginger-haired young man with extensive shoulders and surprising pink fists. 'You're that bloke off the telly. That fat bastard. Comedian.'

'I'm a comedian, all right,' I say, with an empty spluttering laugh.

'Les Dawson! That's it. You're 'im. Well, shit, I'm a big fan o' yours, Les. Put it there,' he says, grabbing hold of my hand.

'Get off me,' I say, knocking his wrist away.

The room is suddenly quiet. All eyes on me. The lad stiffens.

'Steady now, Andy,' says the landlord.

'Right,' I say, swaying, one hand gripping the lip of the bar, my normal voice returning. 'I'll tell you what I do, shall I?'

'Go on, then. What's the big deal?' comes a voice from the pack.

'I'm a social worker. That's what I do.'

'Whoo!' comes a fresh voice. 'Better watch it, lads. Might 'ave come for yer kids.'

'I'm a social worker. That's it. Have been for sixteen years. All that time looking after shits like you lot. And for what, eh? So you can live out your poxy little lives, fiddle the dole, get pissed of a Friday night, go home and belt the wife, bugger the kids . . .'

'I think you'd better shut it,' says this Andy, striking a more solid pose with a half-step to his side.

'Fuck off, airhead.'

'Right. That's enough,' says the landlord. 'Out. Go on. I don't know who you are, but you're going.'

'He's going all right,' says this Andy, smoothing the skin on his thick, nutmeg-downed forearms.

'I'm going nowhere.'

'We'll see about that,' he says, with a confident glare.

But the landlord lifts the flap on the bar, is round in a moment, and, though I am twice his size, he bundles me with ease, feet scuttering, out of the door and into the street.

'Go on. Piss off and don't come back. We can do without your sort round here. Out of it. Go on.'

When he's disappeared back into the pub I'm left squinting at the building, at the waste ground beyond, the sky, the night air suddenly about me like a cold skin. A gang of girls seem to have appeared from nowhere, filtering around me on their way into the bar, their whispers reserved, their laughter shrill northern laughter. I want to tell them not to bother with that place, to tell them it's a shithole. But the words would not be mine and nothing comes, anyway.

I stagger away.

A bridge once crossed.

Somehow I have found my way home, an abiding instinct having guided me as I drove the car haltingly across the town. And as soon as I put the lights on I see my house for the hovel it is, see my own lack of imagination in never having wanted to live anywhere else. A waste of a life. Should have learned to look out for number one. Nobody else would. And I realize I can devise no pleasure for myself here. Not any more. The drunkenness I have not known for many a year only serves to make it worse – I'm at that ugly, ruminative stage. But sleep must come some time. All the sooner, I'm thinking, if I wrest my bottle of gin from under the sink in the kitchen. Which I do, pouring stern insalubrious measures, softened with mere drops of water from the tap. I sip and grimace, then drain each glass. And yet I'm thinking I'm not drunk. Can't get drunk, I'm muttering to myself as I fall back against the cooker and pointlessly sweep a handful of coffee mugs to the floor. I'm a big dumb animal, looking at the mess, stupidly thinking to reinforce my action, pulling at the drawers in the kitchen, forgetting in an instant what I might be looking for, searching for searching's sake, till my hand alights on a small brown plastic bottle of tablets that must have belonged to Angela. These'd do. Few o'these, eh? says the unknown voice, returning with force, filling my head, more familiar than my own thoughts. And I carry the tablets and the gin into the living room where I manage to draw the curtains, having it in mind to drop just two pills, maybe four, to bring on the drowsiness that's eluding me. Then it's a handful I have, swept rattling to the fat maw with a burning swig of gin. A few more, eh? To make sure, pal? A bridge once crossed, though? comes my own weak voice. 'It's not that,' I tell myself aloud. 'Just need a rest. Long rest. That'd be the ticket. Get out of the game. Just for a while.' But the gin bottle becomes too heavy to lift and it's tumbling away with a thump and I'm scattering the tablets like pellets for fowl, feeling leaden all over, looking up at the ceiling, trying to stay awake, focusing on a crack in the plaster that seems to grow and grow . . . and the room splits open . . . and the roof is blown away . . . and Time Itself and God Almighty . . .

The muck curdles in my stomach, fermenting into a whole which comes back in a single bulky expression after which I'm on my knees in the mess, giving thanks to whoever might hear. And all is good, infinitely comic as I pass out, serenely, laughing into a welcoming oblivion.

When I wake it's to a ringing, a single, sustained, far from celestial note in my head. And a knocking too, an intermittent pulse, polite then forthright. Someone at the door. I pick myself up, frowning at the congealing splashes on the carpet, every detail of my stupid behaviour of the night before already arriving to taunt me. Then the knocking begins again and whoever it is seems to know I must be here. Angela? I hope not. Pride alone makes it an intolerable thought that she should see me in this state. I brush myself down as best I can, removing the stained jacket I'm still wearing, pushing my vomit-scaled fingers through my hair. I turn off the light and pull the door shut, quietly, before opening the front door to the brightness of a clear dawn and a blue-suited, fresh-faced young man. Someone, I admonishingly consider, who does not spend his nights trying to drink himself to death.

'Robert Munro?' he asks.

'Might be,' I say facetiously, wondering if something remains of the alcohol in my veins.

'Social worker at the Dale End Health Centre?'

'Sounds like me.'

'I'm Detective Sergeant Garbutt. Local police. May I come inside?'

'Is it important?' I ask with a respectful air. 'My wife and daughter,' I lie, pointing above my head. 'Still asleep, see.'

He eyes me from smile to belly to feet and back again, looking beyond me into the hall, sniffing the faint miasma of booze and sick that must be in there, has to be on my clothes and breath.

'It's about a William Duff,' he says. 'I understand he's one of your cases.'

'I know a Duff. Might not be the same man.'

'We have it on good authority –'

'Whose authority?'

'– that he's one of your clients. And I'm afraid I must insist on your immediate help. You see we know, or rather, we're pretty certain, that last night this Duff – resident at the Albert Hall Hotel, yes? – well, we think he's killed a man. He's wanted for murder, Mr Munro. Is that plain enough for you?'

'It is,' I say. 'Oh God, it is.'

PART 2

At first I'm merely puzzled, the man's assertion being too blunt a fact to admit into my mind. When he asks me if I would go to the police station to answer some questions, I shrug, betraying my confusion. Then I agree, asking him if he wouldn't mind my taking ten minutes to inform my non-existent wife where I'm going.

'Sure. Certainly,' he says.

I invite him into the hallway, knowing I cannot expect him to wait on the doorstep. He smiles with a faint embarrassment, seeming hardly able to restrain his curiosity about my bedraggled appearance, or the glutinous sweet smell by the closed lounge door. I leave him in the hall, hoping that, if he is to be believed, the fellow has murder on his mind and that should be enough to distract him from making any comment about me or the state of my house.

Upstairs I change and wash quickly, catching myself smiling oddly at my reflection in the bathroom mirror. The man's words begin to rearrive slowly in my thoughts, dispelling the residual flippancy of the night before. What has Duff really done? While I was half-poisoning myself, might the lad truly have been in the act of killing – the word thrills me in a disturbing way – someone? Once I'm over the first obscene shock I begin to feel sharp, responsible, hungry for details. I had it in mind to speak a few words to the empty bed, for the sake of the man below, but I decide against it, knowing I would only make a hash of it.

When I return downstairs, it's to find this Garbutt standing in the kitchen by the sink, looking a little pale, broken crockery and the hum of last night's excesses everywhere.

'Bit of a party,' I say, gesturing at the mess. 'And that's not all that was smashed! Well, shall we go?'

He nods with something approaching relief.

In the car he is more relaxed, telling me in polite tones that they think Duff is responsible for the murder of an old man, a shopkeeper, one Buster Gee, a name I do not recognize. I make the appropriate noises of a formal dismay, hardly able to contemplate the things he's telling me. Then he is silent and I'm watching the streets slipping by in the fine light of morning, the world looking renewed, as if on the verge of some great, mysterious enterprise, drawing me into it, a necessary unbelieving participant in this grim adventure.

At the station, where I had imagined there would be all manner of urgency and alarm, there is only a disarming air of tranquillity. Behind the enquiry desk a single officer yawns, tugs at the sleeves of his smart white shirt, nods at Garbutt as we pass. A square of sunlight from the skylight glints on a row of tubular chairs that line the corridor down which we walk, Garbutt leading the way to the office, he tells me, of Detective Inspector King.

The senior man smiles as I enter, extending his hand which I shake too keenly. He's wearing heavy black-rimmed glasses and a brown suit of exactly the same cut as Garbutt's. I catch a whiff of aftershave. On his desk is a telephone, a neat pile of handwritten notes, and a portrait picture of two children. A man of order, precision, a family man. I think we have met before, though I cannot remember the occasion and this would not seem the time for reminiscence. Garbutt guides me to the chair in front of the desk and I sit down awkwardly, my hips filling the thing from arm to arm, suffering, in my mind, the exquisitely unnerving sensation of being the criminal myself.

'Sergeant Garbutt will have told you the details. Yes?'

'Unbelievable,' I say. 'All of it.'

King rests his elbows on the desk, palms joined to give him more the look of a village pastor than a policeman.

'So why? Why'd a lad just walk into a tatty corner shop and start beating the daylights out of a defenceless old man? Could have emptied the till easily. No trouble. Gee wouldn't have put up much of a fight.'

'You're sure it was Duff?'

'The neighbours spotted something going on. They don't miss much round there, as you probably know. Half a dozen saw him running off. One knew him from the dole offices. Perfect description. Landlord at his digs confirmed it.'

I shake my head in a vague, unaligned commiseration.

'You know him,' says Garbutt from somewhere behind my head. 'D'you think he could do something like this?'

'No,' I say, perhaps too abruptly. 'Quite the opposite. Bit of a quiet sort, really. You wouldn't think there was an ounce of harm in him. Honestly.'

King looks down at the papers on the desk. He is not satisfied with my reply and I know it, feeling every bit the naïve social worker, the bungler who may well be held responsible for all this.

'Tell me, Mr Munro, what you really know about him,' says King.

I answer with a contrived zeal, anxious to appear as if I want to be involved in all that's going on, though I have no heart for the game, offering only dry details, certainly saying nothing about my having been with Duff the day before. King listens patiently while I digress on the intellectual aspects of motive, social deprivation, things I know will only bore him. He needs to know, of course, where Duff might be hiding, and he seems more interested when I tell him about the squat, pencilling the address on a piece of notepaper which he hands to Garbutt. I tell him about the Royfix unit, offering other worthless reflections on Duff's poor job prospects. Then I say I can supply him with my case notes which he says he would like to see some time, though I sense no real enthusiasm on his part.

'All that stuff'll come out later. When we've got him,' he says, his last comment sinking in my head like a stone in water.

He suggests we take to the streets, visit the places I've told him about, see if anything might nudge some memory into life, anything Duff might have told me about friends, relatives, places he knew particularly well. Realizing that I might be his only help in this matter, I agree, as eagerly as I can, though I'm only keen to be out of the building, my head aching now with both the desultoriness of the previous night and the surreal awakening possibility of my involvement with a murderer.

Garbutt and another officer are sitting in the back of the car while I am in the front next to King. The Inspector speaks into the radio while he drives, seeming to be directing the movements of other vehicles about the town, giving the addresses of the squat and the Royfix workshop. But I can hardly be bothered to listen, feeling an indignant sense of innocence, an abandonment of the professional responsibility that affected me earlier. Why should I help them? What could be in it for me?

At the squat the two subordinate officers burst through the door with a theatricality that makes me want to laugh out loud. When they return, shaking their heads, King and I enter ourselves, finding only the old wino in the front room. He's different now, quite clean-shaven and soft-spoken, the room having been tidied up a bit, the sofa replaced by a single armchair, a tea chest serving as a table, and by its side a kettle and a camping gas stove. He does not know who Duff is and King believes him immediately, smiling rather kindly at the old buffer, which impresses me. Then we go to the Royfix unit, usually closed on a Saturday, but Healson is there, laughing in the sunshine, talking to two uniformed policemen outside the open main door. Garbutt is the only one to get out of the car, soon returning with the news that the building has already been searched and there is no sign of anything amiss. And soon we are away to the

Albert Hall Hotel where we all file inside, finding the landlord in a sombre mood.

'I'm sorry,' I say to Ally, out of hearing of the men. 'Duff, I mean. I'd no idea.'

'Supposing the mad fucker comes back tonight? What'll I do?' says Ally, wringing his hands, pacing the landing outside Duff's room.

'Tell him supper's off,' I say, unwisely giving the lie to my appearance of concern.

King stalks about Duff's room, looking thoughtfully at the bare furnishings, the peeling walls, the bad air of the place reasserting the picture we all have of Duff – a loner, a drifter, a loser. From an open drawer he picks up Duff's dole card, turning it over, reading the name aloud before he puts it back with an unexpected semblance of respect for the lad's possession. Then he seems at a loose end, to have exhausted all immediate possibilities, to have lost hope that the case might be wrapped up quickly and the hunt might not have to expand into some grander operation he'd rather not order. And I feel fully aware of my uselessness to him, thinking he might soon tell me to go home – the last place, for all my mistrust about this business, that I want to be.

'Maybe if I saw where it happened?' I say, the words tumbling on to the musty air, surprising us both.

Garbutt smiles wryly, but King answers, 'Might help. We're going back there next. You may as well come.'

And soon we're passing through the Rawton estate, a maze of maroon-bricked council houses on the south side of town. Apart from telling someone on the radio about where he was going, King has been silent all the way, and it's my guess that he's beginning to tire of me, suspicious, perhaps, about my interest in wanting to see the scene of the crime.

The shop is soon in sight, cordoned off with gay red and white tapes strung between a bollard, a lamp-post and a Give Way sign at the junction of the road. King pulls up on to the pavement and a bored-looking constable outside the shop door straightens his stance. Thirty yards away a group of boys are playing football on the grass verge and it strikes me how slight this death seems, how unaffected everybody is. Where are the angry crowds? Why are the children not passing by for a peek through the open door? What's the matter with everyone? But there's only a numbness about us all, an eerie calm mingling with the slight spring breeze as we straddle over the tapes and make our way through the doorway.

Then I see it – the tipped-over meat slicer, the strewn shelves, cakes and paper bags, cards of shoelaces and bubble-wrapped toys, a calamity of tinned foods and bottles, a stoved-in refrigerated display case, shards of glass glinting like diamonds on the worn tiled floor, everything scattered in a mad fallen wheel, the terrible evidence of the occasion of Duff's madness. The hairs bristle on the back of my neck, and my face is flushed with the severity, the fact of it all, the thought, now appallingly believable, of Duff's hands at work in creating this mayhem.

'A mess, isn't it?' says King.

I can only nod in benign agreement.

'Our guess is that he came round the counter to start the attack. Hit him in the head, legs, kidneys. Frenzied, that was it. May have had to go into the back room to find him. It's bad, really. Can't believe that it was thought out beforehand. Few murders ever are. Accidents, the most of them. Mostly in the home, too. But then you'd know that, wouldn't you?'

'Would I?' I reply, unable to look away from the scene, less shocked now, taking in odd details of the things which have remained undisturbed – a row of sweet jars behind the counter, a display of cigarettes, an old stool in a corner beside the big refrigerator.

'Something must have got into the lad. Can't have been the money. Friday, see. The old man always went to the bank of a Friday afternoon, the neighbours said. Probably no more than fifty quid in the till. And Duff left the change. So what had upset him, Mr Munro?'

'I don't know. Can't think,' I'm saying, discovering now, with a returning dismay, the chalk marks on the floor and the lumpy scattering of sawdust used to cover the black puddle of blood behind the counter.

Feeling faint, I tell King that I'd best be off, that I'd like to go straight round to my office to consult the notes I've made about Duff. I'll be in touch as soon as I think of anything new. King seems hardly to have heard me, saying that he thinks it'll not be long before they have him. His men are scouring the town now, and it's not a big place, as we both know. He offers to get one of his officers to drive me to the health centre, but I decline, walking out of the shop and away without another word.

But I had no intention of going to the office. Rather, I walked away from Rawton, veering back round the suburb's boundaries, half a mile or so till I reached a road that would lead to my own street. Then, back in the house, I paced through the rooms, smoking, smiling in my own solitude and dissembling incredulity, opening windows to let out the winy stench that had permeated into every corner. For a while, an hour perhaps, I sat on the toilet in the bathroom, thinking of nothing. Then I set about cleaning, first the mess in the lounge, then the whole house, from top to bottom, an activity that took most of the day, increasing in tempo and range, and for which I seemed to have a boundless energy.

If there is a God I certainly had Him, or a god of sorts, in mind that day I saw Duff's handiwork in that shattered old shop. It occurred to me then, concerns me now, that there might be a divine quota of some kind – a celestial register, perhaps no more than a rudimentary stock list (laugh, if you like, I can quite see the funny side of it myself) – and that somehow the violent death of the old man, the extinguishing of his life in this crude and uncalled-for way, had at the same moment reasserted my own existence, staying the hand I might have taken against myself. It's a romantic idea, and goodness knows this is not the place for fancy-led notions, but I couldn't help thinking it then, considering now the possibility that Duff, in cruelly wresting the last breath from Buster Gee's pathetic body, had saved my own life.

It was a sobering idea – literally, at the least. And, for a while, the whole incident subdued me, made me stop thinking about myself for once.

I sleep most of the next day away, my dreams, such as they are, coping happily with my problems without interference from me. In one I'm on a stormy sea in a leaky lifeboat with Angela, Sandy, and a shady figure I cannot put a name to. Angela is frantically trying to bale the thing out, while Sandy attends indifferently to some blemish on her bare stomach. For myself I'm laughing, telling Angela she need not be so scared, that the water's only two feet deep. I'm about to jump over the side, eternally in this position, though I never do, preferring to taunt Angela about her futile efforts. In another dream I'm sitting in a hotel lobby, abroad somewhere, with Rycott, arguing, repulsed by the idea that he wants us to go up to the room we are to share, where there is only one bed that will have to do, he says with a suspicious indifference, for both of us. The foreign – Italian? – waiters and bell boys circle, knowing the situation, mocking my discomfort. And in another I'm seven years old again, walking through our old village with my father who takes my hand, leads me up to the church and shows me his own gravestone. It's from this, I think, that I wake, late in the afternoon, shivering with the cold.

I rise only for a couple of hours, fixing myself a huge meal, a mess of anything I can find – sausages, tomatoes, peppers – of which I eat perhaps a third while I'm sitting in front of the television, watching the local news.

At first it seems that Duff's crime has not merited reporting, having been eclipsed by the news of another murder in the county. A naked young woman has been found stabbed to death in a jacuzzi. She'd been listening to her Walkman, a George Michael tape, the presenter's saying. Until a few months before she'd been an assistant in a meat wholesaler's. Then she married the boss of the firm who has now gone missing. The story is loaded with innuendo – a handsome victim, a fancy bathroom in a big house (over a shot of which the story is related), George Michael, husband a butcher, of all things. I chuckle to myself when I think of the jokes that will circulate in the bars tonight about not eating the meat pies. Then, in a twenty-second slot at the end of the bulletin, I see Inspector King, solemnly stating the tragedy of Buster Gee's murder, and of the need to find one William Duff who may still be in the area and who could certainly help with their enquiries. The familiarity of his voice disturbs me, and I'm up on my feet when he warns that the fugitive might be dangerous and should not be approached by a member of the public. What does he think Duff will do? Whose sensibilities is King trying to preserve? Oh, but the smugness of people, the righteous of this town, this society. When the news is over I picture one of those scenes outside a police station with Duff being bundled out of the door under a blanket, rubbed along through the crowd who are baying and howling, celebrating their relief that the beast who has threatened their comfortable, meaningless existences has at last been brought to book. It's an ugly anger I'm feeling, an old pain that's stirred by all this, even though my rational thoughts inform me that if and when Duff is caught, there'll be no such interest. Old man Gee's death will draw none of the sympathy undoubtedly aroused by that of the pretty young woman. I look again at the scene I have imagined, see that it has developed sensibly to the dreary office of the crown court, me among the thin attendance, winking at Duff, if I cannot help myself.

Towards evening, feeling monumentally heavy and listless, I return upstairs to a dreamless sleep, troubled only by a recurrent ring of the telephone which I do not answer.

'I'm glad,' says Rycott. 'Glad you came in. I was worried.'

'Worried?'

I take a few steps towards my desk, not certain, in this intricate hiatus, whether or not the gesture of my removing my mac will give Rycott the advantage. I could still just be visiting to offer the last notice of my intention never to return here, darken the doors, the like.

'When you didn't answer my calls. It's been five days, Robert. And not a word from you.'

'Three. Three days. And, anyway, I'm not in the habit of ordering my life to sit by the phone all day, waiting for the damned thing to ring.'

'No. Of course not.'

I remain standing, close to Malcolm who is seated at his desk, sniffing, writing notes, manfully trying to ignore the situation.

'You wanted to see me about something,' I say to Rycott. 'Last Friday. I got the message.'

[137]

'A few things cropped up. You've no need to worry. Not now. They'll sort themselves out, given time. There's just the one case that's pressing.'

'Oh?'

'Do you think we could discuss this in my office?' he asks, nodding openly at Malcolm who can only return a blank, loose-mouthed stare.

'What's wrong with here?' I say. 'Anyway, which of my blunders is bothering you now?'

'I'd rather it were elsewhere, Robert,' Rycott says, the merest, lilting hint of firmness in his plea.

'Here. Now.'

'Very well,' he says, folding his arms, leaning back against a year planner on the wall. 'Duff. William Duff. I gather the police have been to see you.'

'Called round for me. Saturday morning. Taxi service. Film star treatment.'

'And what's the situation now?'

'No idea. Haven't heard the news this morning.'

He pauses, leans forward a few inches. 'Listen, Robert,' he says, carefully. 'You're not to blame for any of this.'

'Oh, I get it now. You mean the department's not to blame.'

'All right. If you like. I just want you to know that I think we should stick together. I don't want anyone carrying the can alone in my patch.'

'It's District, isn't it? They're after you. They're after all of us. Right?'

'That's not quite the situation. No. We've a thousand potential William Duffs on the books, and we all know it. It's happened in the past and it was going to happen again, some day. On this occasion you were the one involved. All I want, Robert, is for you to stick with the case until there's a result.'

'So I can cop the consequences personally?'

'We're behind you all the way. You can count on senior management support.'

'Don't make me laugh.'

'I need you, Bob.'

'Is that what you wanted to tell me last Friday?'

'You're not helping any, with this attitude.'

'That a fact?' I say, but I'm trembling in the sight of a rare and spontaneous victory. And to press my advantage further will only serve to dilute it. I take off my coat and drop it on the filing cabinet, answering the unspoken question that has troubled us all in this room. 'All right, I'll stay.'

'Good. I'm glad to hear it,' Rycott says, immediately assuming his usual calm authority.

'But there's nothing I can do about Duff until the police have found him.'

Rycott is already making for the door. 'Just do what you can, Robert,' he says. 'What more can any of us do, eh?'

I sit down at my desk as the door closes.

'F-fuck's sake, Robert,' says Malcolm. 'You h-handled that well. B-bloody well.'

'Did I?'

'T-too true.'

'I've lost, Malcolm. That's the reality. I'm letting them get away with it.'

'Oh c-come on, Robert. O-only last week, y-you were in the sh-shit up to your eyes.'

'Still am. The truth, see. It'll find us all out in the end.'

'O-oh?'

'You're lucky, old mate.'

'D-don't follow.'

I'm about to tell him that he's past his crisis, that I've had troubles of my own lately, some of which I might perhaps unburden on him. But he's tugging at the roots of his beard now, shoulders rounded, looking boyishly, impossibly vulnerable.

'S-so?'

'Nothing, Malcolm,' I say. 'Forget it. Good to be back, eh?'

'R-right,' he says, smiling warmly. 'M-missed you, Robert.'

'Thank you, Malcolm. And I missed you too. Now, we'll get on, shall we?'

'S-sure. We s-sure will.'

For the rest of the week I went about my work as before, though my heart wasn't in it. I was marking time, waiting for something to happen, for me to be, yes, victimized in some way. It was true that the Wakefield boy had been lying and had been returned to his family and Rycott happily gave me the news that Brittan was not going to press charges against us for fear that it might complicate the appeal against his last conviction. But the fact remained that I was to blame and I ruminated badly over it, wanting to be made accountable in some way – such a hunger I was developing for this deliverance, in whatever form it might take. As for old Maisie, there was no word from the hospital and each day that went by reduced the likelihood of anyone pursuing the matter. It was just one of those things, they'd be thinking. It happens. Duff, though, was still on the run and it was my secret belief that he might have taken his own life, that he could well have been in the river, his body slender pickings for the pike. It would seem fitting, appropriate to the way I knew him. And the longer it went on, the more I recalled my dealings with him, seeing him in different shades of light, letting an image of his crude features – teeth, eyes, hair – expand until I could think of nothing else. Though if he was alive, what could he be thinking? What part of this dead and dreary town might his fugitive's eyes be watching?

I kept my thoughts to myself, letting them trail after me as I went listlessly about my business. Of all the problems on our

[141]

hands, Duff was my case. He belonged to me. My boy. And I needed him to stay at large, if only for the diversion it caused, for the way it kept at bay that greater waiting sadness, that dark hole that faced me when my working day was over and I was at home, alone, the loneliness inside me pressing against my scarcely conscious being like some urgent question trying to form itself.

So the weekend arrives and I have no hopes of spending it as fancifully diverted as the last. I have risen late, shaved, showered, even though there's no one to impress with my careful appearance. I try to think how I used to spend my time before Angela, going through the routines of doing my washing, vacuuming, fetching a morning paper, forcing each task into the framework of time I know it used to take me. But there's no familiarity, no pleasure now in these innocent tasks. I have been changed in some way. Things are not as they were. I feel old, very old. And who is to blame? How can I say it's Angela's fault? She was the innocent one. And I envy her for it, despise her, engaging in solitary conversations in which I'm explaining to her the pain she's caused me, reasons, solutions, appearing perfectly defined, always with the same concession – that I forgive her, that she must come back. Now. It's morbid, I know, but it fills the time, soothes its chafing passage. Then there are no more words and I find myself – as if coming across my own person in the street – standing in the kitchen, staring out at my back yard, thinking it could do with sweeping, saying so aloud. But I've no appetite for the task, nor for any more of the trivial activities with which I once whiled away my weekends, as I counter each new idea I can think of with reasons for not doing it. Then, without any conviction or plan, I lift my coat from its lonely place on the hooks in the hall. I will go out. I will walk. Anywhere.

I select no particular route, drifting naturally towards the town centre and its focus of Saturday afternoon activity. The streets are vapid and damp, a faint mist clinging to architecture and the people alike, none of whom I know. I, the one who cares, the fat man who once forgave the shortcomings of all others – socializing has never been his strong suit. But then that's always been my way, my problem – I thought I was above all that, passing private judgement while I offered absolution, not wanting to believe that the people here are for the most part happy, have a capacity for it, a genius for seeing out their days without saddling themselves with the moral burdens I gleefully sought for myself.

I walk on, passing a steamy laundrette, the Methodist church from where I hear the last few lines of a doleful hymn, the teeming supermarket where the customers file with their rattling trolleys, each having about them a functional, necessary air: families to provide for, must get on. Ahead of me I spot a knot of people on the pavement, a tumble of whites and pinks, blues and browns, a petalled cluster on the grey steps of the town's registry office. I slow my pace, half hoping that they might have dispersed by the time I reach them. But the crowd seems to have thickened even more when I get there with tepidly smiling onlookers among whom I can only stand, unable to pass them by.

A photographer bustles his way to the front, standing perilously close to the passing traffic. 'Let's be having a few smiles, then,' he challenges. 'Bugger me. Supposed to be the best day of your life, this.'

'An' it's all downhill from now on,' calls a watching woman, drawing cackles from her companions.

The groom forces a nervous grin, showing a gold-crowned front tooth. His bride smiles defiantly. And the women around me sigh. 'Pretty enough,' says one. 'Can't be more than eighteen, mind,' says another.

'One more for your gran,' says the photographer, taking three more shots before waving his hand in a dismissive gesture. Then, as one body, the party gathers itself together and hurries off along the pavement, the men taking to the flanks of the crowd while the women hold on to their hats, stepping on discarded cigarettes with the points of their white shoes. And they melt from the grey of the day into a line of parked cars, returning in our direction and away, the ragged cavalcade being swallowed quickly by the sweep of traffic rushing from the town.

Around me the women who have been watching seem at a loose end, saddened by the end of this small event, offering occasional quizzical glances in the direction of the fat man, the only man, who has been watching with them. I feel the same improbable sense of loss before I go on my way, round the first corner I see, to free myself of their slight curiosity.

I follow the incline of the street, between frowning rows of high Victorian terraced houses, to the alley at the bottom. From here I have the choice of either crossing a car-park to my left or following the gentle curve of the alley which will eventually lead to another street and the riverside walk to the town centre. There's no choosing, though, just movement, as I walk on down the centre of the alley, looking up at the white strip of daylight between the high walls of the houses. I can hear water running into a gutter in one of the yards behind the walls and from a lofty open bedsit window there is the erratic progress of an argument between a man and a woman. The air is cold here, one of those places where the daylight never seems able to penetrate and the cobbles are forever moist. I look back, taking a chilly pleasure in my solitude, in the sense of enclosure that the alley affords. Further on is the wall of an old warehouse, its black and purple bricks bulging perilously. Then there's a filmy wash of yellow ahead, a detail of daylight which I discover comes from a missing section of the building. When I reach it I find a complex still-life scene of scaffolds, ladders, ramps, ropes, wheelbarrows, a dusty idle cement mixer, the only figures in view being four young men.

At first I take them to be workmen employed in the task of either demolishing or refurbishing the warehouse – it's difficult to tell what is meant to be going on here. Then I see that they are like me, trespassers with no business in this place. One of them is asleep on a hardened clay banking. Two of the others are working quietly about him, shushing, giggling, pressing a makeshift wooden cross into the ground above his head, easing a few scrawny flowers into the hands clasped on his chest. The fourth, an older man, is standing ten feet away, watching the proceedings with a quiet detachment. No doubt all are fresh from the pub, killing a few hours before the evening session. I turn to pass on my way, knowing, though, that they are certain to spot me – a figure my size does not slip inconspicuously across such a static prospect. And I have gone twenty yards when I hear the foulmouthing behind me. I glance back, fatally, to see that the sleeping one has woken and is chasing the others with the wooden cross raised like a sword. Then they begin in my direction, inevitably drawn by the curiosity of the only other flesh and blood in sight. I do not, cannot run.

'So, what's this, then?' says the first to fall in step with me.

He smells of port and earth and there are dried dribbles on his T-shirt. A second youth takes up at my other side, imitating my walk, making me mortally conscious of my waddle, my fat man's assailability. Then the first man wheels out in front of me, holding his hard hands against my shoulders.

'In a hurry, then? S'the rush? Little lady wife waitin'? On a promise, are we?'

'No,' I say, my head dropping.

'Fat enough,' says the other. 'A right porker.'

'It's a fact,' says the one in front, his breath steaming, drops of dew in his ruffled hair. 'Fat get like you could do with exercising. Get some of that lard off. Eh?'

He rips open the front of my coat, tearing two buttons from the fabric, the meat of his mouth up against my nose. Then he grabs the folds of my stomach with his steel-hard fingers. 'Look at this! Look at all this,' he says, wrenching the flesh agonizingly. 'Too many puddings. Fat arsehole. Too much feedin' your fat fuckin' face.' He pulls me around till my feet slither on the cobbles and I stumble free of his grip and on to my side, a bolt of lightning shooting from my hip where it makes contact with the ground. A pause. Then a wiping of the wet lips before the other man unexpectedly delivers a boot to

[145]

my back, a fist to my temple and another to the back of my head. Instinctively I wrap my forearms about my skull, with a stray, risible thought in my mind for the landlord of the Black Dog who rescued me the last time I was in a situation like this. But I know there's nothing I can do. No saving me now. 'Let's roll 'im!' comes the voice of the third youth who has now arrived hotfoot behind me. And they begin pushing me along, heaving me on my back, then on to my stomach, ten yards or so before they stand back wheezing with obtuse laughter. 'Look what you've done to us!' says the one who began the assault. 'We're fuckin' knackered now!' But the third, who has more energy than the others, takes a number of steps backward in a measured arc from the crumpled half-conscious heap that I have become. 'Stand by!' he shouts, scraping the ground with his boot. 'Two points comin' up!'

But he is stopped, quietened by the older man who has idled up to us, who comes over and looks down at me, a roughhouse professor inspecting some weak and unsatisfactory specimen. I see him through a glazed veil, hardly able or willing to open my eyes. 'Do it,' I whisper, tasting lead with my tongue. 'Finish me off. I want you to.' He comes closer, grins, showing a row of worn, nicotined teeth, a calm expression, a street-born and weary sapience I have come across before. 'What's that?' he says. I squint up at him, through the heat of my pain. And I laugh, despite the hurt it costs me. Him. Of all people.

'S'you, innit,' says Brittan. 'Fancy that.'

'Small world,' I say, struggling up to my knees, then falling back on my side.

'S'your lucky day, fatso,' says Brittan, softly, out of hearing of the others. 'Your fuckin' lucky day. You owe me somethin', fat shit. You owe me plenty.'

'I owe you nothing,' I say, vainly trying to stand again, making it only to my hands and knees.

'Fer two pins I can see to it you never walk again, bastard.'

'Do it then,' I say, sitting back on my ankles, my head folded into my chest. I see his fist against the front pocket of his jeans, curled hard as a rock inches from my face. 'What's stopping you? Deserve it, don't I?'

I look up at him, seeing the simmering anger behind his concentrating features, a warring of indecision and restraint. Then he backs off towards his wearied silent companions, pointing a stubby yellow finger at me. 'Next time, fat boy. You got it comin'.' He nods to the youths to follow him away. 'Enough. That'll do. For now.' And they trail after his jaunty denimed shoulders, troubling him with half-urgent enquiries about who I might be and why their sport should be so disappointingly ended.

And later – when I have dragged myself home, doubled over, attracting, wanting the sympathies of no one who passes me by, revelling in their looks of fear and distaste – the process begins. And it's as if some ancient compound has been released into my bloodstream and I'm cosseting my passivity, treating myself to my humiliation, smiling, thinking of my whole ridiculous history, of my family, gathered before my open believing eyes, the events that have buoyed me up here in this exquisitely lonely present, the undeniable present: Duff, Rycott, Maisie, Brittan, the thousand others whose lives I have tainted, they're all here, the crowd appalled by my laughter, baying my name, coming for me, tripping me up, laying into me, fist after fist, boot upon boot, but they can't hurt me. Nothing hurts me now. I'm easy sport. So easy they can't touch me. Because there's no one here. I'm no one now.

Sleepless. Nerveless. I was, undeniably, out of myself. Even the aches and pains of the assault on me seemed to belong to someone else, though I had a vague idea of feeling grateful for the attack, as if I had brought it on myself, wished it as a token attrition for my follies.

At work, my injuries aroused a veiled concern. I was attacked, I said. And I certainly had no intention of reporting the matter to the police, I added, defying any further enquiry. The incident itself became totally diminished in my mind, an unacceptable part, perhaps, of the process of my . . . My what? My madness? Was that the way I was going? Was that to be it? Life over? End of story? It was a giant possibility, but one which I accepted calmly, with a blunt resignation, as I went about my business over the next few days. There was, simply, no way back to being the man I was. Or, at least, had always believed myself to be.

So, it's a Friday and I have spent the morning assisting in the removal of a few old mental cases from the local hospital to a nursing home, no one around me aware of the storm building and raging in my head. I now work without conscience, without despair even, only a wistfulness, an outward treasonable contentment guiding me through my days. At lunch-time, back at the health centre, with no one to disturb me, the decision is made, arriving with a razory clarity, dissipating the stasis and dream-like quality of all the accumulating hours and days. I shall walk out of here and I will not come back. There's to be no fuss, no drama, no telling of the reason why I am to take my own life. Let them find a solution for themselves. It will not be the right one. But who cares?

I walk out of the door and through the empty waiting room, half-saddened that there is no one there to bear witness to my smile which has, I think, a singularly tranquil quality now.

Outside, the sun is baking the tops of the cars and the day has taken on an opaque feel, each new second seeming quite impenetrable. It's the right thing to do, and I know it, though the details, the wherefore and how I shall actually perform the deed, have yet to arrive. I know only that this time my intentions are clear.

I walk out of the health centre car-park, ignoring my own vehicle, seeing this as the first part of the act, an intriguing detail they will have to consider when they try to trace my last movements. On the busy road a juggernaut rumbles at my own pace, teasingly close, and I eye its wheels with fondness, admiration. But it's not right. Not here. Not like that. I drag myself on a few paces and then along two side streets. Then, without quite realizing how I got there, I'm standing in the bar of a pub I've never been in before, marvelling, yes, at the way I now seem to have lost all control of myself, at how I am now so innocent. The process is complete. I did not want to come here, had made no plans for it, had no say in the matter at all. I'm quite delirious, in that compartment in my head where this last part of me resides, hovers, is almost gone. All about there is smoke and laughter and life in all its harmless glory and it wants nothing to do with me. Alone at last! Till the fruit machine behind me wakes me from the dream, spewing out coins to the squeaky delight of the woman in front of it. It's a voice I know, I'm thinking. 'Angela?' The name escapes curled round a soft gasp and I'm feeling faint, on the brink of some new and appalling embarrassment when I look round, turning only half-way, seeing the soft white hand scooping the silver discs from the machine's mouth, the same unruly hair, the dear, dear warpaint.

'Angela?'

'S'up, fella?'

The eyes tell of a genuine fear. She sweeps the coins into her handbag, letting them drop loose inside.

'I'm sorry. I thought you were someone else.'

'Nah. I'm me, pal. Only me.'

She contrives a hard glare before tottering out of the room to the lounge bar where I see her talking to the barman, pointing in my direction. He comes through and I take a step towards the bar, a movement again hardly of my own choosing.

'What you after then?' he asks.

In this half-light, he looks like me, the way I believe myself to look, the same deadened eyes, the overfull mouth with plaintively downturned corners, the peaky nose, tiny chin, soft jowls, the bottom teeth of which you see too much. It's not a face that you'd want to see too often, that you could greet with pleasure. Then I think I really am looking at myself, seeing once more the whole of my life, the coming, the going, the standing still-ness of it all. Pointless. The lot.

'Well?'

'Nothing,' I say. 'You can't help me.'

He shakes his head, turning away from me to snatch glasses from the bar, plunging them into the sink below. And the spell is broken. I rub my eyes, my face. Leave.

Back outside the world looms large and reminding again. I'm angry with it, with the way it insists on its own importance, the way, yes, it is ignoring me in my last hour. I should not have to suffer this. Someone, somewhere, should know about my passing. And suddenly the time-scales both in the noise that wheels around my ears, and in this tiny space in my head, become confused, colliding, crashing together in the most dreadful mix. I walk a few paces on, shivering in the sunlight. I take a cigarette from my pocket and light it, each movement slow and stiff. But I don't want the thing and I let it fall from my fingers to the pavement, walking on with some purpose now, as the shape of my final scenario suggests itself and I know what I must do.

*   *   *

Ten minutes later and I'm driving fast, but with a dour control, across the town. It's a long shot, I know, but one I must try.

I am not too late, it seems, as I find a convenient stretch of road to park opposite the entrance of the Friarage School. Outside the low-roofed modern complex of classrooms the buses stand in a long silent row, their drivers beside them, having a smoke. Then there's some activity as boys appear in the road, as if from nowhere, weaving on their bikes, blazers flapping, rucksacks swaying on their backs. My heart gives a little as the girls arrive next, walking, impossibly pretty in navy and white, gawky faces, three-quarters adult. I get out of the car, anxiously searching among the itinerant expressions. The one I want, if she is here, will not be like these – she will be introspective, bored. Alone, I fancy.

But it's not the case. When I see her she's tossing back the long hair, smiling brightly. She's with a friend, laughing now, thumb trapped beneath the bag strap on her shoulder. I cannot remember seeing Sandy as a schoolgirl before, and it makes me feel uncomfortable, reminds me how little I really knew her, how small my claim on her mother might be. I take a step towards her as she makes to cross the road.

'Sandra?'

She looks at me, feigning surprise. And I'm thinking she's already spotted my car, has, somehow, been expecting my arrival. 'Oh, Bob,' she says. 'What're you doing here?'

I take hold of her arm to communicate what I can of my restlessness, to make it a fact, let it be known.

'Where is she?'

'Bob,' she says, tugging against my grip. 'That bloody hurts.'

'Your mother. Where is she?'

'Don't think much of your boyfriend, Sand,' says her petite, pale companion. 'Dirty old men now, is it?'

'Robert, please let go of me,' Sandy says. 'People are watchin'.'

'Tell me. Go on. Where are you staying?'

Two more girls join the group, one tall and thin, the other seeming half her height, plump, with a ruggedly sculptured peroxide perm.

'S'goin' on, Sand?' asks the fat one.

'Nothing. It's all right,' she says, pulling herself free with a sharp jolt.

'What's your game, fella?' asks the tall one, grimacing absurdly.

'Shut up.'

'Watch it,' says the fat one as other girls slow their pace about us. But I'm mindless, careless of the idea that I'm now causing concern – the hot disturbed middle-aged man, alone at the school gate, openly inviting the girls' voluptuous wrath, their bristling self-righteousness.

'Better fuckin' leave 'er alone, mister,' says the tall one, nervously wiping a shank of hair from her forehead, checking around her for the support she can count on among the gathering crowd.

'Get in the car,' I say to Sandy. 'You're going to show me where she is.'

'Not goin' with 'im, are yer, Sand? More sense 'an that, 'aven't you?'

Sandy shakes her head vacantly. 'I know him. It's all right. Honestly.'

'You wanna watch yourself, love,' says a passing woman, laden with shopping, stepping forward to take a glancing interest.

'I know what I'm doing,' Sandy says. 'Though I don't think he does.'

The group's concern seems diluted by Sandy's assertion, but they hang around still as she follows me to the car and gets in, watching all the while as I pull out among the exhaust fumes of the revving buses, bumping and stalling my way through the writhing bodies of the departing youths.

'She'll not thank me for this,' Sandy says primly.

'I'd have found her. One way or another.'

'Don't know what good you think it'll do.'

'I'll worry about that. Just show me where to go.'

Five minutes later and she's waving her fingers at the ends of two roads of cream-rendered bungalows.

'Not that one. The next. If you're sure you want to go on with this.'

'I'm sure. Which is the house?'

'One with the yellow door. I'd better go in first. She might not want to see you.'

'I'll decide that.'

I park hurriedly, at an angle, in the first space I can find, waiting impatiently on the hot pavement while she drags out her bag and swings it up on her shoulder. I follow her down the garden path to the door, feeling quite nauseous with restraint while she puts her key in the lock, turning to offer me one of her maddeningly knowing looks before she pushes the thing open. But I can't wait, brushing past her into the hall and on through the first door I can find.

Here, in the picture window light, a television soap opera tune is blaring loudly at an empty, plum-coloured sofa. On the wall is an Indian rug. There's a smell of herbal cooking. And by the old range fireplace there's a tray of dirty coffee mugs. Then there's Angela, appearing from the kitchen, before me like an apparition, someone I can hardly recognize at first.

'Bob? Jesus.'

'Tried to tell 'im,' says Sandy, entering behind me.

'Well. Fancy,' Angela says, with an uneasy, watery smile.

'I . . . It's good to see you, Angela.'

But I'm standing this small painful distance from her, hardly able to contain myself, the time-scales slipping in my head again. I can see her there, feel our old association, a curious idea of her having been my property, of her having stolen her doll-like presence away from me. Then it's as if I've never had any real possession of her, as if her body is merely an instrument that she used precisely, cruelly against me. She's smiling but I can't believe in its authenticity. She's from another race, another species whose laws I do not understand, whose morals are lower than mine, whose every manoeuvre is designed to exclude me and to trash my feeble dignity.

'An' it's good to see you, Bob.'

'Things have been bad, Ange. Very bad. Going wrong,' I say, all I can retrieve of my many rehearsals of this conversation.

'What? Work an' that?'

'Yes, work. No. Not that. Just . . . everything.'

And then all changes again, in one simple movement, in the stirring of my muscles as I slip round the armchair that's between us, fists clenched with a tension that's immediately reduced, disappears in the fraction of a second it takes for me to cross the boundary from my society to hers, to put my arms heavily around her, to force my nose and lips into the warm hollow between her neck and shoulder, to pit my weight once more against her weak resistance, to know that faint miasma of soap and old perfume, to possess again, more than anything, that warmth that stays all thought, changes me for the thousandth time this day. And Sandy's going 'Oh my God' behind me but I don't care, can think of no force on this earth that could keep me from this touching, this knowing of someone else.

'Bob. Please. S'not so simple,' Angela's saying, pushing demurely against my hold. 'Come on, Bob. Let go.'

'Can't. Don't want to, Angela. Need you. All of you.'

'Bob . . .'

And then I realize we are not alone, the three of us. Not as before. Another body has entered the room and there's a sudden stillness, a barrier to any further exchanges. I turn around, stumbling and cracking my elbow on the wall, Angela taking the opportunity to slither from me and across the room while I'm steadying myself, quite unable to contain a single cough of hollow laughter.

'Tell me. Say it isn't.'

'H-hello, R-Robert.'

'I m-meant to tell you, Robert. B-but the moment, see, it n-never seemed quite right.'

Now all time has stopped and my humiliation before the three of them is out, completely unadorned. Malcolm is standing to my right. Dumb Malcolm. A weak and mixed-up man. But he's a winner today, with no apparent sensitivity, no feeling of debt for all I have done for him. If there's a second in all my forty-three years when I have witnessed human insensibility at its most despicable, this is it. I look up at the ceiling, down at my shoes, my breath light and faint, a too familiar heat in my cheek as I struggle with my temper, trying to preserve it in some way, though I know my energies are failing, withering away. At last I say, voice faltering, 'Maybe you could tell me how long this has been going on?'

'W-well . . .'

'Not so long,' says Angela, looking past me to some high empty angle of the room. 'Malcolm came round wi' some benefit forms for me.'

'You were at my house?'

'Y-you were out s-some place. Y-you always took the d-difficult stuff on yourself.'

'And look how you've repaid me!'

'S'not his fault,' Angela says. 'You don't own me, Bob.'

'I d-do regret not telling you, Robert.'

'What fucking good's that? And I suppose,' I say, pointing at Angela, 'you're going to tell me he just threw himself at you?'

[157]

Angela says nothing, biting at her thumbnail, looking near to revealing some secret fury of her own, a sample of concealed truths, perhaps, that I know I might prefer not to hear.

'M-m-maybe I did.'

'It's no good trying to cover up for her, Malcolm. There's nothing you can tell me I don't already know about her,' I say, immediately regretting my words, my failure to obey the fear that she will round on me.

'Oh?' says Angela. 'An' what's that? Go on. Say it. I'm a rough piece. A friggin' tart. That's it, innit?'

'Have I ever said that?'

'No. But it's what yer think.'

'I did a lot for you, Angela.'

'You did a lot for yerself. It was all for your benefit, my comin' to live with you. What was your game, eh? What were you playin' at? God or somethin'?'

'That's not the way it was, and you know it.'

'I-if I c-can say a word . . .'

'Oh shut up, Malcolm!'

'There's no need to talk to 'im like that. S'time you realized you're not who you think you are, Bob Munro,' Angela says, shaking, half turning away as if she too cannot bear the thought of the revelations she might make. But I have an appetite for it now, a calm, growing need to have my fate delivered to me, articulated in full.

'And who am I then? Go on. Fill me in. I'd like to know.'

'I th-think Angela's t-trying to say you're t-too idealistic, Robert.'

'The fuck I am.'

'P-please don't m-make things more unpleasant th-than they n-need be.'

'He's right,' says Angela. 'I think you'd best go, Bob.'

'Go where? To do what?' I say, grumbling out the words as I make for the door. 'You were my life, Angela. The lot. There's nothing else.' I pause before leaving, knowing only too well the bridges I'm burning even as I turn to face them again. 'How could you? Both of you?' But they can only look away in embarrassment, wanting me to leave, as so many people I know have wanted my lumbering presence out of their simple lives.

And so I'm away into the sunlight, the anger sparkling in my head as I wrench open the car door and sit, beating the steering wheel with my fists, all pain and bitterness, all life's paltry meanings draining away.

I died, then. That was the last of me.

From the dormer window of the bungalow, Sandy impassively viewed my mad display and watched me drive off. I had it in mind to end it there and then, I think, to slip the car into the river, perhaps. But an emptiness opened up before me, a great capacious house of nothing. I could not take my own life without some awareness of what I was doing, some intelligence carefully drawn to its most perfect and durable pitch. There must be a reason for all this. And there had to be justice, a levelling of scores. It was a childish notion, I knew, a hubris of the most catastrophic order. But I had a right to take my revenge, to experience in my last hours one moment of true selfishness, to simply and cleanly collect all that was owed to me.

So, it's the next morning and I'm lying in my bed, clumps of sheet gathered in my fists. Outside, somewhere nearby, there's the unearthly clatter of a road drill, its hammer taps reverberating madly against the windowpane, mingling with my hazardous thoughts. But I'm feeling a queer sense of happiness, as if this is the first day of a long holiday and I have only one small duty to perform before I am released of my burdens for ever. The wall before me in my mind is insurmountable. There's no turning away from it either. My mind's made up – all it took was a hair's-breadth shift of moral emphasis. I want to hurt. To cause damage. I want to kill someone. Simple as that. The deliberations have been made, the night spent reinforcing a notion of the worthlessness of human flesh, of its inconsequentiality in this world, in this universe and all its infinite reaches. I will go back to that house and take the life of whoever I find there. Simple as that. It will be a crime of passion. Common enough, these days. Widely celebrated in our films, literature, songs. And there'll be a logic for all to see – the spurned and jealous lover, driven to distraction – which will take the edge of pointlessness from the event. It's Angela I'm after, I know. But she may not be there and time, and the enthusiasm I shall have to muster for the assault, may not permit me to be too choosy. And certainly I have no intention of seeing out the rest of this day. No more of these empty nights. No more caring or forgiving. Especially not the last. No. Today I live my last hours and I live them for myself.

I rise and shower, formulating the idea that I might be able to carry out the murder with some dash. If it's Malcolm I'm to struggle with, it might be difficult. Though I fancy he might just lie down and let me . . . What? How am I to do it? I laugh to myself, thinking that in all this time spent willing myself to this conclusion, I have not spared one second's thought for the way in which I am to kill. And what if there's only the girl at the house? Such a young life . . . But I'll not stop to consider the ethical arithmetic. Not now.

I select my clothes with a heady precision – a worn white cotton shirt, jeans which will not hang half-way down my backside, suede boots: the uniform in which I am to be discovered. And each action of dressing imparts a new dire certainty, a confidence born of the fact that it is to be for the last time. As for the means by which I am to dispose of myself, I envisage only that there will be such a heat inside me, such a delirious revelation that is said to be the experience of one who has just murdered, I shall either slip beneath the wheels of a passing bus or it will indeed be the river, though the notion that I might have to witness the recollection of my entire life – famously the experience of one in the act of drowning – is a sufferance I'm none too keen to bear. It's a detail, though, this how and wherefore, and I scarcely pause to consider it. The last moment will bring its own answer, when all is done. All settled.

In an extraordinary moment of pure calculation, in answer, it seems, to someone else's bidding, I put on my mac and go into the shed in the back yard to select, yes, a hammer from my scant collection of tools. And once again it's another being who's guiding me, who inspects the angry-looking claw on one side of the tool's head, tries it for weight, exercising his wrist with the thing. And then, briefly, bitterly – this I'll confess – I'm weeping, seeing in this small action how far removed I have become from the life I once knew, that seems happy in retrospect, tantalizingly recoverable. And a single image of childhood, of myself at eight years old running home from school, troubles me and I'm that child again, knowing and wise, shaking his head at the foolish ways of the adult I have become. But I force the memory away and drop the tool into the inside pocket of my coat.

I return to the house, eyes smarting, barely able to look round for one last time, knowing how procrastination will eat at my resolve. Outside, the drilling has stopped and I have only a silence with me, a tranquillity that seems too precious, that might stay my hand if I linger too long. I make a routine inspection of the windows and close the back door as if I'm going to work, the ritual making me feel easier, calmer. Then I pass through the hall and lock the front door behind me.

I dispense immediately with the idea of taking the car, feeling instinctively that it has no part in the plan, the awful scheme that seems to be taking shape of its own accord. I shall walk there, make myself visible, let anyone who might want to bear witness after the event see my troubled expression – I have nothing to hide, no pretence of secrecy to make.

A drizzle is misting the pavement, fine, northern rain, cooling my cheeks deliciously. At the opposite side of the road, a little way down, is the old man who has been operating the road drill. He's alone, flitting manically about the generator which is silent now, seeming to have broken down. He pauses to watch me pass, taking off his cap and smiling oddly as if he knows my business, my folly, the whole pathetic history of my life that has led me to this day. I try to ignore him, continuing on to the end of the street and down an empty avenue where I see, on the horizon, an absurdly dramatic, almost religiose flash of sunlight illuminating the white silos of the liquorice factory. I stagger a little, trying to control my trembling fat body, telling myself that to faint here and now – though no more than anyone would expect of me – will do nothing to help my cause. I consciously tense my limbs and force myself onwards, considering the details of my route, sublimating, if only for a while, the true purpose of my journey. And the time passes raggedly, each step taking both an age and no time at all.

Soon I'm at the market, the true heart of the town where everywhere there's the fetid reek of meat and fruit and the houses round the square look sombre and beautiful, black gables scowling down on the canvas roofs of the stalls, on the cobbles strewn with fruit wrappings, trampled beer cans, torn flapping boxes around which the old people perilously two-step. And I hear, suddenly, the cries of the traders ringing out on the air as if cheerily heralding my arrival. But the shoppers seem on edge, reserved and despondent, as if they have sniffed out my tension, my steely malignant cause.

At a stall decked out in greens and reds and yellows a young woman with a child in a pushchair is turning a cabbage round in her hand. 'Bet it's full of caterpillars,' she says. 'Aw, love,' says the man behind the stall. 'Wouldn't pull a trick like that. Not on the best-lookin' woman I've had all morning.' She snorts. 'Save it for the old ladies,' she says, putting the cabbage back, forcing the pushchair away over the cobbles. I stand watching her go, as if this is a scene from a film, inexplicably convinced she is about to cry over this trifle. 'And you, sir?' asks the man. 'What can I get you on this fine morning?'

I look at him, at his grimy expression, feeling angry.

'Well?'

'Nothing,' I say, walking abruptly away, dismayed now by every scrap of inane conversation around me, the empty humour, the wheedling refrains. I walk out of the market and down a narrow street where the rain is falling in twisting silver columns. And I'm feeling newly dispirited, energy trickling away. A drink, perhaps, would be the thing. Two, maybe. Just enough to induce that gruff melancholy to which I have become partial of late, that gravity beyond moping that should ensure I go through with the task I have set myself, coward that I am.

The wind lifts the flaps of my coat, presses on my shoulders like the arm of a pitying friend, and I shuffle along with a growing sense of ignominy, acutely aware that I am soon to bring more suffering, greater calamity to add to the centuries-old air of defeat that the people of this town have to breathe. But then maybe I'm thinking above my station – they'll forget me soon enough, perhaps will ignore the whole business from the outset, the way they have ignored Duff. This idea lifts my will and I press on, wiping the wet from my cheeks, wondering if I have been crying again. I cannot tell and it hardly seems to matter.

And now I can see the Black Dog, mighty and alone, just opening, my old friend the sour-tempered landlord bolting back the doors. He does not look at the round wet figure who is making his way towards him, and I'm wondering if he'll recognize me. I press on, hoping that he will and that, for whatever reason, he will show me the same quaint hostility as before.

Here, then, I seek my final sanctuary. It's as good a place as any. And at least there will have been a witness, someone no doubt only too willing to help those who might wish to trace my last movements. I shall make it easy for him, drinking recklessly like the last time, swaying dangerously, being deliberately noisy. Good. A good thought, yes, something to give extension to my resolve. This I'm thinking, thinking still when I stop dead on my feet, hardly able to trust my eyes as

I look out over the stretch of waste ground behind the pub, spotting the thin figure that's picking its way over the muddy arena between us. The lad looks up, stops, sweeps the wet blond hair from his forehead. And even at this distance I can see the grey skin drawn over the goofy teeth. The wind soughs heavily. I smile.

PART 3

In the draughty space that separates us, a hundred yards or so, there is nothing but surprise. I call out, waving at Duff as if to an anxiously missed friend, but he ducks from his direction at an angle, scurrying quickly to the rubbled edges of the muddied landscape.

I see no signs of urgency, no swarms of uniformed policemen with yapping dogs, descending from the town on their quarry. And I hear no sirens in the distance, only the muffled rumble of traffic up on the main road. Shouldn't I now turn away to the door of the Black Dog? I have no argument with Duff, for all the gravity of his sins. And, besides, are we not both soon to be guilty of the same appalling transgressions? I feel a fragmentary stab of envy, or perhaps it's humility, since the fellow has already done his deed, and quite without the performance and ritual I'm bringing to my own efforts. Murder. It's in the air. Everywhere. The cult of it, the appalling thrill of its very name! Oh, I'm laughing all the while as I begin following Duff at an unaccustomed trot. Imagine the sight! A middle-aged roly-poly, haunches wobbling, trying to skip round the puddles, slithering like a duck on ice. The would-be assassin. And when I reach him, what shall I say? Am I after commiseration? Advice? I have no idea, save that I might want him to be the last person to have seen me in possession of my senses and to let him know that, yes, I forgive him for all he's done. No one else will, not a soul on this wretched earth.

By the time I reach the far side of the waste ground Duff has disappeared into a side street. I follow, finding the pavements deserted, an opening at the far end the only place he could have gone if he has not entered one of the houses. I stumble into the alley, disturbing a stray dog from a spill of litter behind a yard door. At the end is a car-park where I see him again, standing by the nodding barrier, waiting for a gap in the traffic to cross the road. He is still too far away for me to judge anything of his expression or intent, though from the quick visible plumes of his breath I get the feeling that he has about as much appetite for pursuit as I have. Maybe I should leave him alone, recover the fatefulness, the delirium of my own day. But I'm drawn by him, stalling in the no-man's land between idea and intention. He starts running again, dodging haphazardly between the hesitantly progressing lorries, vans, cars cramming their way to the town centre. Then he's shambling away down the first street he finds. I walk on, quickly as I can, my breath coming a little easier now, my heart seeming to have engaged in a new and unexpected gear.

At the end of this street of smoky-haloed back-to-backs, there's the road that leads left to the station and right into a tunnel that runs beneath the railway lines. I cross over and on towards the tunnel – guesswork, a fifty-fifty chance – but there I see his skeletal silhouette. He hardly seems able to keep a straight line, shouldering the wet tiled wall, stooping, stumbling over his feet. I call to him, some weak strangled word that comes out belonging to neither this nor any language. But he simply puts purpose into his lame trot, not bothering to turn round, already out of the tunnel and into the picture of light at the far end. I begin running again, the sound of my footsteps compressed and metallic.

When I reach the end the distance between us seems to have neither diminished nor increased. Surely someone in a passing car must be able to see what's going on? A double decker bus comes swaying by, its passengers ghostly behind the steamed windows, boys huddled in rugby scarves, a punk-haired girl watching, but seeing nothing unusual in a bedraggled, middle-aged man's pursuit of a limping, wraith-like youth.

Up ahead Duff almost collides with a young woman and when I reach her, seeing her face stern and smarting with the rain, I feel almost as if I should apologize on the lad's behalf. But I only smile, saying nothing, resuming my leaden canter to where Duff has veered away down a rough track towards the old railway sidings.

Now I can only walk along the grass-tufted lane, reaching the abandoned yards some minutes later. Here I find a long, graffiti-splashed concrete block wall, the ground a moonscape of dumped tarmac and cement, tangles of rusting wire sprouting from the earth as if in evidence of some vast spent machine beneath. 'Bill? Billy?' I shout into a spray of rain. 'Come on. Let's talk, eh?' But there's no answer and I wonder if he has at last given me the slip. 'How's about showing yourself, Billy? What about it, fella? You've worn me out, dragging me down here.' A goods train rumbles past at the other side of the concrete wall, its growl easily defeating my words. Then I see Duff's head, emerging from behind a derelict brick shed thirty yards away. In the teeming rain I hold my arms open wide in a gesture of conciliation. 'What about it, Bill? Want to talk? Can we do that? Mates, aren't we?'

He shakes and rolls his head like a wearied lover. In his hands is a crimson bundle. He fidgets with the thing, ripping at it until he has revealed its content – a beautifully obscene black toy, the one object that could lift this day to the heights of a truly hysterical insanity. A gun.

'Aw, get wise, Billy. I can't fucking believe this,' I'm saying, to myself alone, certain that the thing cannot be real.

From the railway station, a mile away, the platform announcer's voice blows in on the wind, swirling eerily about the spaces of the yard. I squat down, forearms on knees, sensing no danger, merely a heightening sense of absurdity. And I laugh.

'Away, Billy! Having me on, aren't you?'

But he's aiming the thing at me, holding it double-handed in the falling English rain, a pose fraudulent to the point of whimsy. Then he's backing away, stumbling on a hillock of clay and grass.

[169]

'Stop,' he yells, when he's back on his feet. 'Stop fuckin' followin'. Got no argument wi' you. Just bugger off. Leave me be.'

'All right. That's all right with me. Just take it easy, eh?'

But he starts skipping sidewards, slips on to his knees, and is up again, making for the wall. When he reaches it he tosses his black gem over before straddling the concrete himself, needing three terrific pulls before he reaches the top then falls to the other side.

I stare into the space he's left. A few moments to think, to try and accept what has taken place, wondering how it is supposed to fit into the scheme of this fantastic day. I blink skyward, the rain thinning to a drizzle, the wind flapping in the high ivory void, whipping the clouds into horsehair. In a few hours' time, I am meant to have killed, to have become a martyr myself. But this plan, its monumental design, seems already beyond my grasp. It's as if I'm viewing it as a past event, as if this distraction, the time it has taken up, has moved me on in some way. It's as if, yes, it has already happened and yet its victims have survived and, indeed, have known nothing of their murder. It's a massive exaggeration. It has not taken place at all. I feel suddenly heavy, tiresomely mortal again. Now I shall never kill, shall for ever carry the burden of their sins against me. Oh how the days will drag, how I shall ruminate, suffer, let it eat me away, atom by atom. Too much. The thought of it is all too much to bear. I take a few steps forward, dragging my sodden boots out of the sucking mud, reaching firmer ground. Today there will be an end of sorts, I'm thinking. And Duff will be part of it, somehow, a means, a vehicle, incredibly, divinely provided by the kindly religion of coincidence. I begin walking with some purpose, doubling back out of the yard and along the other side of the wall then through the swishing wet undergrowth towards the river and the direction I think the boy might be taking.

And now, since the words are coming apace, I'll pause no more, not while the same winds rattle the windows of my poor little house, send the litter flying to the roof. No, I'll not even bother with the knock at my door that I can hear at this late hour. It will be no one, nobody other than some poor beggar I might once have known, seeking my help, foolishly realizing nothing of my duplicitous ways, of the Judas kiss of my altruism. For him, whoever it might be, I can offer no help, no relief. Those days are over now and I'd say it's for the best. This I'm thinking now when there's an end in sight, a conclusion to be offered from which I shall not flinch. I'll get on. Should get on. I'll have the courage for this, if nothing else.

So . . .

I find the river brown and swollen with the rains, the water swirling back and forth, its progress wilful and random. A few people are hurrying along the bank tugging wet manic-eyed dogs behind them and I look for urgent expressions, signs of terrible dismay, any clue that these people might just have been face to face with, God laughingly forbid it, a gunman. But there's none and I carry on, a sharp stitch in my ribs, towards the blue block contours of the town, that skyline that draws me back, binds me to itself again to entwine both our inglorious fates.

At an iron footbridge I stop, leaning against the mossy stone of an upright. Away in the territory I have just left a lone express hurtles along the horizon at breakneck speed. I breathe deeply, my exertions catching up with me as I feel in my mac pocket for a sodden packet of cigarettes. I light one. Good time for a smoke, this. Deserved. I feel instantly calmed, watching the river dividing itself around a buttress of the bridge. I've been here before, I'm thinking, recalling that when the patients of an upstream mental hospital take to the water, this is where, two days later, they come to the surface. I found one myself, once. An old man, still wearing a blue summer suit, his body among the reeds, head nodding horribly. No one I knew.

I throw the last third of the cigarette into the water and force myself on, along the path that leads up to the town, past a playing field where a football match is starting, the players with their sleeves stretched over their cold fists. Further on I reach the first houses, detached, with long lawns and rockeries, conservatories, wide bay windows – expensive places where my social work services were never needed. Then, when I'm close to the town centre, I turn away from the river and into a park where the wind comes in snatches, baring the pale undersides of laurel leaves, snatching petals from straggling white roses. Hikers have emerged into the warming light and umbrellas are being shaken, human life reasserting itself after the rains. And there's no sign of disturbance, no rent, no spike in the peace of this place. If Duff has passed this way, no one has noticed him.

I sit down on a bench, looking up at the clearing skies, down at my knees, my eyes closing, dry as paper. And the old thoughts depress me again with their dead weight. What could I really have been thinking about when I started this day? I feel in my inside pocket and pull out the hammer, testing myself for what might remain of my original intention. No one notices as I toss the thing into a litter bin, smiling wryly. This act, unselfconsciously performed, imparts a sense of relief, a rare occasion when I have forgiven myself. My madness of scarcely an hour ago is now no more than a memory, a silly sad fact to add to the thousands of others which, compounded, have made up my forty-three years. Today I'll kill no one. Another twenty-four hours in which I have not murdered.

I open my eyes fully, an irrepressible good humour upon me. And I'm thinking in a practical way now, about Duff and what might have driven him from his hiding place. Might he have been walking the streets all this time, these fourteen long days? It wouldn't surprise me – he's so slight and unremarkable, so much a part of the sub-life of this town that he would need little luck not to be spotted. But the gun was unexpected. I can hardly believe in its authenticity, certainly not in the idea that he has it in mind to kill again.

Two minutes later and I have joined the weekend crowds

in the shopping precinct. Now I'm looking nowhere, ambling along, gazing dully at windows full of pine furniture, second-hand clothes, reject china, a shoe shop from where a whiff of leather combines with the fat fumes of an adjacent Burger King. I'm a man doing the town, a dishevelled, tired old creature in need of a rest, a long sleep. I look straight into the eyes of a passing constable, silently daring him to guess what has been on my mind, with what murderous intent I woke this morning, what comical alliance I had made with someone he should be looking for. But he does not rise to the challenge. He's just a fellow doing his job, innocent as the rest.

Back in the market square I go into a café where the warmth further induces my lassitude.

There are no more than half a dozen people at the round tables, each poised above a cup of coffee, seemingly in search of the same forgetfulness as me. I'll sit among them, let my coat and shoes dry, allow my head to empty of all thought. But at the counter I spot a young woman from the refuge, a client of mine, sitting with another woman I do not recognize, shopping bags leaning against the legs of their table. I order coffee, irked by the fact that I shall not be able to avoid them as I make my way to a place by the window. I pick up the cup and saucer, worrying about my speech being incoherent.

'Hiya, Robert. All right?'

'Yes. Fine thanks . . .'

'Ju.'

'Of course. Julie,' I say, quite unable to remember why she had been referred to me.

'You workin' today? Bob's always workin',' she says to her companion. 'Told you about 'im, didn't I? Proper saint, our Bob. Got me out of a fix.'

'No. Not working. Just up the town. You know.'

'Not out chasin' that lad, then.'

'What?'

'You know, the one as did old man Gee in. I come from the street where it 'appened. 'Orrible business. Saw your name in the paper.'

[173]

'I'd rather forgotten about him,' I say, lying easily. 'Police matter now. Dare say they'll find him, soon enough.'

'Ange not with you?'

'No,' I say, this cold truth offered with a lesser facility. 'Not today.'

I turn my back on her and cross the room. Now I'm feeling an insipidly returning sense of duty. The holiday's over. I really should be doing what is expected of me – dashing about the streets in a police car, directing the driver to where I had discovered Duff, where I think he might be now. If it comes out that I have seen him and have not reported it, my life will become instantly complex again. And I'm thinking I do not really want that now, that I have energy already for putting the past behind me, getting matters straight again. But I'm tired, very tired. Soon. I'll see to it soon. I rest my sore feet on the rungs of another chair, light a cigarette and stare out of the window. And the scene I'm looking at has an extraneous quality, as if it's a protraction of one of my dreams, the shoppers going about their trivial business, traders laughing and cajoling, welcoming the sunlight. And there's an unnerving freshness about it all, a healthy certainty in the bricks of the houses, the blue sky above, in the faces and voices of the people whose aspirations I can once again only guess at. The man, the I, who passed by less than an hour ago – hammer in pocket, one foot poised above the grave – hardly seems worth thinking about now. He was someone else, someone I might never understand again. Then suddenly the peace of the scene is broken and there's an urgent truth in the air, the raincoated bodies scattering with the pigeons – people and creatures abruptly animated by a sound which, like me, they cannot quite believe in. A gunshot. Then another. And twice more.

In the square, no one seems quite sure where to go or how to behave. A few, roused by some ancient instinct for survival, run to the four corners while others shuffle along, shaking their heads, looking to each other with blank expressions of denial. A woman in a smart tweed coat seems plainly irritated by having been disturbed from her shopping habits, moving nowhere, still offering money to a stallholder who waves her away. The rest of the traders stay where they are, behind their goods, like press-ganged infantry nervously guarding their lines. For me, time reassumes its now familiar refined quality, and I'm equal to it, feeling an acute sense of self-control. I stand, watching the scene more closely, believing myself to be a part of it, to have had, somehow, a hand in its conception.

It looks as if the shots have been fired in a nearby street, though they were certainly loud and recognizable enough. In the next half a minute people drift into the café, pausing in the doorway, looking up at the blackboard menu as if trying to intimate that this is where they had been meaning to come all along. But they're shaken, I see that. And their eyes and universal pallor betray the fact that they are seeking a resumption of the peace in their lives which, until now, they had conceitedly taken to be eternal. But that was in another time, a world that existed before the advent of big bangs. They stalk the room quietly, hats in their hands. One man even orders tea. Others join me at the window, mumbling at my shoulder.

'Church Street. That was it,' says an eager youth.

'No. Away up the library. Some place round there,' says an older man.

'Could be nowt,' says his lady companion. 'Fuss over nothing.'

The rest seem to want little to do with looking out of the window and I wonder how many of them might be trying to connect this with Duff, how they might be thinking of his name. Sirens begin sounding in far-off streets and a fire alarm goes off in the square, unsettling the confused peace that has descended in the last minute. Then a white police Escort skids on to the cobbles, the first, almost exhilarating sign of something happening. The car's driver speaks out of his window to one of the stallholders who shrugs expansively, pointing to the skies before it reverses furiously and speeds out of the market. A few of the traders gather in a knot about the man who has spoken to the officer, looking about the square, daring glancing inspections of each others' bemused scowls.

In the café the tension has become untenable, the general air of bewilderment sloughed away as people begin speaking in low, respectful tones. I feel large, awkward, hot. It has to be Duff. But what history is the lad trying to invent for himself? If I go out now and bump into him, might he open fire on his social worker, seeing in me a flesh and blood symbol of whatever it is he's fighting against? I stir myself with a massive conscious effort, pushing my way through to the door.

Outside, the atmosphere seems unexpectedly relaxed, almost weirdly festive after the sickly warmth and enclosure of the café. They're assuming the worst is over, I'm thinking, that nothing can happen to them now the patrician hand of the police has stirred in their defence. Men holding pints of beer have gathered in the doorway of the Market Tavern. Women and children appear from the cold shadows of the houses, blinking in the sharp light, come to do their shopping. Already the incident has been reduced to a forgettable anecdote. I go over to the man, a fishmonger, who spoke to the police officer.

'Well?' I ask.

'They think he might be up by St Mary's. Wanted to know if we'd seen him here. That's all,' he says, roughly rearranging his stall, seeming uncomfortable with the tiny celebrity afforded him by the situation.

'Have they any idea who it is?'

'Plain, isn't it?'

'Is it?' I say, not wanting to trust in his speculation, reluctant to have the fact out in the open. 'Anybody hurt?'

'Dunno, fella. That's something we'll have to find out.'

I walk away from him, meandering between the stalls, then away up an empty street that leads to St Mary's church.

When I arrive I find no signs of anything untoward, no marshalled ranks of police officers, no gunboy fighting them to the last man. On the church forecourt a pavement artist is working quietly. A dustbin wagon and its workers are making their way slowly along the road. By the vicarage a soft breeze loosens the blossom from a lone cherry tree. All is as it ever was. I am disappointed, excluded from the drama of which I feel I should be a central part. I go down a paved street of antique and art shops, but can find no sign of activity, no agitation in the dry, dreary Saturday peace. I walk more quickly, wondering if Duff might not have done it to himself by now, that the only scene I might discover will be in a back snicket, police officers huddled over a blanket-covered lump on the ground. It would seem the likely outcome. But then, as I'm making my way to the busier streets on the edge of the town centre, I spot a sudden movement, a tumult of bolting figures at a crossroads a hundred yards ahead. I begin running towards the mêlée, turning a corner and following its elusive progress to the end of the street. Here I find a recreation field with unoccupied swings and a ghostly still roundabout. Beyond this is a Victorian infants' school, a lofty-demeanoured red brick heap with high narrow windows, through the doors of which a century's children have passed and where, now, a swarm of policemen is scurrying to its playground boundaries like animals to the wire of their cages.

[177]

A constable arriving at the end of the street sees me standing in the middle of the road and comes across. 'Do yourself a favour, mate. Be off, eh?'

'It's Duff, isn't it?' I say.

He looks at me warily, irritated.

'We're clearing the area. Now.'

'Tell me it's Duff you're after. I'm Bob Munro. His social worker.'

'And how'm I supposed to know that?'

I pat my pockets for the identification card I haven't carried for the last ten years. 'I know King. If he's here, I want to see him. I might be able to help if I knew what was going on.'

He turns away, waving his hand at two boys on the opposite pavement, a gesture which they immediately, sheepishly understand means they must go back up the street. Then he looks back to me, nodding towards the school. 'Duff's banged up in there. Got a gun.'

'I'd gathered that,' I say, receiving the information with a shock which I manage to conceal. 'Has he hit anyone?'

'Not that we know of. Not yet, anyhow.'

'What's that supposed to mean?'

'Got a kid with him. Snatched her off the reccie. Little bastard.'

'Is King here?'

'Better be, by now. They're gathering round the front.'

'Use your radio. Tell them I'm on my way round,' I say, quietly astonished by my own authority and presence of mind. The constable purses his lips ruefully, advising me to keep my head low, saying I'd best be who I say I am.

The sense of an event is everywhere. A police Land Rover rolls off the camber of the road, mounting the curb at an angle. Two men are working briskly, cordoning off the adjacent streets and alleys with the same red and white tapes they used outside Buster Gee's shop. With dismay, I notice an ambulance edging its way quietly to half-way down a street where people have gathered on the doorsteps, arms folded, to watch the scene develop. In the middle of the road outside the school gates is a sergeant, central to the operation, a stubby radio in his hand. He sees me, seems to recognize instantly the shabby look of the social worker, and waves me over.

'Munro?'

'Yes.'

'Over there. Through the boys' entrance. First room on the left. Look sharp and keep quiet.'

'Is King in there?'

'Go on. Fucking move it.'

I cross the road, pass through the open gates and up the steps. In the corridor I find a policewoman who directs me into an office. And this room is alive with a controlled, anxious activity – careful instructions being offered to the uniformed men who arrive behind me with radios and electronic equipment, cigarette smoke hazing the air, plainclothes detectives sharing out important-looking pieces of paper. Away in one corner is a woman in a flowery cotton dress, fragile among the suits and uniforms of the men. She is silent and her familiar, numbed look suggests to me that she is the child's mother. A policewoman offers her a cup of tea which she takes with a heroic smile. I nod at King who acknowledges me coolly, beckoning me to one side of the room, away from the child's mother whose smile falters in this same moment and who irritably taps away the offered, consoling hand of the policewoman.

'Well,' King says. 'Seems we've found your boy.'

'Where is he?'

'Round the back. Got into one of the portable classrooms. Be pretty simple if it wasn't for the kid. Heard about that, have you?'

'Anyone spoken to him yet?' I ask, ignoring his last remark and its pointless implication of my responsibility in this affair.

He pushes his spectacles carefully up the bridge of his nose. Sniffs. 'No.'

[179]

'Anybody hurt?'

'Seems not. We're hoping to be lucky on that score. Apparently he went into a chemist's shop for something or other. Goes over to the shelves and just starts filling his pockets. Course, the assistant challenges him and he pulls out this gun. Starts panicking. Runs into the street, firing it anywhere.'

'Where'd he get the thing?'

'No idea. Hardly important right now.'

More men arrive in the room with their electronic hardware, their expressions colourless, reserved, as if they are glad only to have this small physical responsibility in the operation. The Inspector ignores me for the moment, exchanging quiet words with one of his officers. I try to hear what they are saying, but learn only that the talk is of a tentative strategy for surrounding the school. I begin to feel a little sick, wondering about their intention to use force, about the sound of gunfire which I heard for the very first time this morning – a sound which pierced straight to my subconscious – and which I may soon hear again. How much noise those lumps of metal could make. How they could wipe William Duff from the face of the earth. On the wall behind me is a noticeboard with fire regulations, cleaning rotas, and a yellowing school timetable – evidence of the aspirations of education, of the hopes and dreams we must inspire in our young. How naïve and misguided all that seems in this moment. But my thoughts are halted by a radio speaker which crackles into life on the worn varnish of one of the tables. The voice whispers its name, Phil, and says it has taken up position behind a green gardener's shed. King makes a slight gesture, overlaid with a meaning I cannot decipher, to his men. The child's mother is ushered sobbing from the room. King half turns towards me, the green eyes concentrating behind the thick glass of his spectacles.

'Are you going to speak to Duff?' I ask.

He seems to be ignoring me, as if to assert his authority, and one of the three plainclothes men around him offers a look which implies I am speaking out of turn. Then King says, 'We've a choice, have we?'

[180]

'I'd like to come with you,' I say, trying to keep any suggestion of enthusiasm out of my voice. 'Might be able to help. You never know.'

'We're going to need all the help we can get, Mr Munro. Come on, then,' he says, addressing the men around him. 'We'll see what he's got to say for himself, shall we?'

'Yes,' I say. 'Yes,' again out of turn, as I trail the four men filing out of the door.

The sunlight is bright, drying the black patches from the tarmac of the playground. Beyond the school gates policemen in thick navy jumpers, pouches slung from the canvas belts about their hips, are quietly unwrapping rifles brought from the rear of the Land Rover. A dog van has arrived. And a policewoman has been posted at each physical corner of the area. Are they armed too? Or are the guns just for the men? I follow King and his three aides as they skip quickly down the steps, keeping close to the maroon brick of the main building. At the corner they stop to exchange some broken breathy talk which I do not listen to, my attention being taken by the goings on, the fuss, the peculiar artlessness of it all. When they suddenly crouch down, I too stoop without being prompted, feeling foolish as I ape the ridiculous waddle with which they make their way to two more men who are squatting behind a concrete play tunnel. King touches one of them on the shoulder and the man nods gravely.

Now we are all looking at one of two isolated portable classrooms which, with a white pebble border round its base, has a curiously cheerful look, like a holiday home or a house made from a toy building set. The door is open a few inches but the blinds are drawn at all the windows. One of the first men here turns to look at me, leaning his head back uneasily against the curve of the tunnel, his hand in his jacket pocket as if he's holding a revolver there that he does not want me to see. His colleague, unshaven, younger, pays me no attention. 'Hasn't made a sound,' he whispers to King. 'Terry thinks he saw a shadow at the second window on the right.'

'What about the girl?' King asks.

'Dunno. Nothing. Fucking nothing.'

'Well, according to the caretaker, there's a fire door round the back. But it's locked,' says King.

'That's useful.'

King settles himself down, his back to the tunnel, speaking quietly and evenly into his radio, ascertaining that five of his men have taken up position behind the far railings of the playground. I watch him, thinking again of the photograph of his children on his desk, wondering obscurely what he must tell them about his work. Then, when he has stopped speaking, there is only the soft breathing of the other men, an almost unbearable silence when I dare to look out past the classroom, not wanting to think about Duff, not daring to believe that he is there, so near, that he is responsible for all this activity, that I myself may be made accountable for not having reported seeing him earlier. At a distant conifer-lined bowling green I can see tardy players being ushered away by the same officer who directed me down to the school. They file into the clubhouse, drawing a stab of envy in me, a wish that I were one of them – blameless in this and every aspect of their dealings in life. A yellow lorry flits between the chestnut trees that border the edge of the park, and I crave either to be its driver or to be magically transformed into a stowaway hiding out among its cargo. I glance up at the clock on the octagonal tower above the main school building. Twenty past one. That's all. Time slowing to a halt, made viscous and meaningless by this awful tension. And then there's a new twist to the induration of time as the sinews and fists of the men around me harden. A hand is pulling at one of the blinds in the classroom. The girl's head shows above the sill. And behind her is Duff. Stupid, dumb Billy, the ghastly white face, the hair in a cap over eyes half-closed with exhaustion or ferment. He's resting the gun on the girl's head, just thirty yards away. But it's his face at the centre of everything, the eye of the mad, silly storm around us.

King leans forward, whispering into the radio. 'You seen him?'

'Bit difficult,' the voice comes back. 'He needs to lean forward another foot.'

Behind and above me I can see a half-open sash window with a short black nozzle resting on the sill. Look, Billy, I'm thinking. See what they've brought for you. Men with guns. They want to kill you, blow your face off, waste your skinny arms away. King tells his man to stay relaxed, both impressing and appalling me with the coolness of his voice. What judgements is he making? And on whose behalf? Is he really thinking that the only solution is to kill Duff? Is he wondering who might mourn for him? The girl, of course, is innocent. Her life is at risk. And Duff's existence has no comparable value. That's the way he will have to think, the way we must all believe, calling to mind only the crudest idea of the purchase of flesh and blood. I look at the other men for some sign of their motives. I'd swear that if the situation were not so serious they might be enjoying this. I feel it keenly, with a stirring piety that lifts me above the sequence of events. I'm wistfully, curiously aloof, and yet still a part of the adventure, struggling consciously with the idea that I might seize control in some lunatic way. I cannot bring myself to look at Duff, feeling suddenly that the whole affair focuses on me, that I am its true centre. 'What do you reckon?' I hear myself asking King, my whispering voice quite detached from the dim rage in my head. But he says nothing. I force myself to look at Duff who seems to be having trouble keeping his eyes open, rubbing them, turning his head in two small circular movements. Then he retreats from the window, leaving the girl where she is, the lowered blind resting against the back of her head. And now that she is alone my thoughts are human again, full of anguish. She is so close.

King resumes talking into his radio with thick local accents coming in reply – other officers apparently seeking more advantageous positions about the playground and among the architecture of the school. A megaphone is smuggled up from behind and for one tantalizing moment I'm holding it in my hands, genuinely believing it's for my own use. But King gives me a withering look before he lifts the megaphone from between my fingers. He fiddles with a switch on its side, giving the lie to his calmness with a grimace of frustration when he cannot get it to work. He hands it to one of the men who twists a second tiny knob and hands it back. Then King shuffles forward, resting the megaphone on the shiny surface of the tunnel, aiming it at the classroom.

'Can you hear me, William Duff?'

I get this in echo, as if the apparatus is sucking King's voice from his throat. He pauses to spit dust from his lips. Then he continues.

'William? I want you to listen to me very carefully. I don't want to rush you, but if you let the girl go, unharmed – unharmed, think on – if you let her go now, then we can talk about getting you out of there too. There are ways round this sort of thing. Do as I ask and we should be able to work out what one of those ways might be. I want you to give me some indication that you understand. All right? William Duff?'

Something is going to happen. Nothing will happen. The girl, perhaps called by Duff, disappears back into the room. The men allow themselves to draw breath. The whole town seems to relax momentarily before renewing its concentration.

'What's the fucker up to?' whispers the younger, foremost man.

The next minute hangs long and empty. I'm aware of the distant murmur of the liquorice factory. Somewhere a dog is barking. Now the town is not listening to us, turning its dull-witted back, snubbing this grotesque comedy. Things like this do not happen round here. But now, suddenly, it must listen, must give up its groans and mumbles in deference to a much more powerful sound. An explosion in the classroom. A cube-shaped boom that deadens the hearts of all the watchers.

And now we want the reversal of time, a chance for redemption, the absolution of all our sins, our many mistakes. A thin black line curls from between King's lips and along his cheek. Among the men there is a chaos of silent perception and disbelief, the air a raw vacuum in the ensuing confusion. Now all thoughts of justice and revenge are in temporary abeyance. Duff's presence is greater than all of them, forcing them beyond assumptions. I alone am the one with a cool head, my thoughts still frozen in those few moments before that awful sound. I'm wanting to tell them that Duff never meant all this to happen, that he's not really evil. None of us are. A little coercion is all he needs, a tiny friendship that is something only I can offer him in this glacial moment, this speck of time when I'm standing and walking towards the classroom, drawn to the flame, the silly habit – I think I've mentioned it before – of a lifetime.

I dare not look round, knowing the despair, the contempt I must be galvanizing in the men behind me. If they saw my expression, the smiling face of a crazed opportunist, I might not be able to resist their anger, though I feel singularly glad to be leaving them behind me, almost exquisitely true to myself.

'Munro! The fuck you playing at, man?'

But King's voice only serves to heighten my elation as I cross the tarmac, beneath the warm and empty skies, to the door of the classroom.

I concentrate on the satin metal of the door handle, almost there, the blood coursing light and feeble in every cell of my shivering body. Am I happy now? In the last few seconds before I reach the door, my action becomes more truthful, wakes me to a new stratum of reality. I try to think of the girl, to become nobility itself. But I'm afraid I shall laugh out loud if I think too much. I pause on the second step up to the door, taking a single deep breath, resisting the last temptation to look behind me, satisfied with seeing King's reflection, his head above the play tunnel, in the glass of the door which gives easily against my touch as I enter the building.

Opposite, the electric light is burning in an open toilet. On the low cistern 'Jen luvs Mart' is scrawled in black felt pen. To my left are rows of pegs at waist height, empty save for an occasional coat and a vivid orange gym bag – the weekend leavings of forgetful children. I stall in the silence, aware of my large physical presence in this place for small people. There's a whiff like spent matches in the air and the light is dull and unshifting. I slowly ease open the door to my right, to the weaker light of the classroom itself.

Sitting at a desk is the girl, a tiny creature wearing a cartoon T-shirt, a pink plastic watch with a face as wide as her wrist. She might be waiting for the next dreary lesson in that bored-looking pose. Her eyes are so still. She can hardly bear to look at me. Then her head nods. She sniffs. Alive. And yes, yes I am glad, mortally relieved.

By the sink to my left, grey and native to the light, is Duff, not bothering to look at me, his indifference an almost tangible attendance in the room. To his side is a scattering of plaster and a long arcing wound in the wall which I assume the bullet must have made, adding the further assumption that the gun – a big, old-fashioned-looking pistol – went off accidentally. He is nursing a wounded hand, opening his shaking fingers to look at the messy red flesh, closing them again. I take advantage of his self-absorption and go over to the girl. I pull at her arm, but she resists. Shock? Frightened of the strange fat man? I smile at her as best I can, stroking the blonde hair tangled with pale blue ribbons, cursing myself for my lifelong inability to communicate with children. She jerks away from me, her eyes still and unseeing.

'Come on, love. You're going back to your mum.'

In the corner of my field of vision, Duff stirs, blinking, as if he's just realized my arrival. He seems larger now, a genuine threat, and he's raising the gun, pointing it at me, looking more practised, more authentic than the last time he did this.

'She goes back now, Bill,' I say, not looking at him. 'You can do what you like. You're not stopping me.'

'Nah. She's stayin'. Mebbe you could both stay. Could do wi' some company. Been a bit lonely lately, I 'ave,' he says in a voice I have not heard before, derivative, full of the hard-nosed certainty of some of the youths of the town. He coughs a short laugh, clutching his side with his injured hand.

I reach for the girl again and she yields to this second touch, standing and sidling round the desk like a miserable pupil being brought to make some confession of guilt to the class.

'I know 'ow to use this,' Duff says.

'Looks like it,' I say, turning to face him, nodding at the scar along the wall.

'Mean it . . .'

'Oh, shut up,' I say sharply, surprising us all.

I put my hand heavily on the girl's tiny shoulder, easing her forward, pointing sternly towards the door, hoping she won't spoil our progress by crying. She walks slowly across the room to the light of day at the open door. She hesitates – silly girl! – testing the floor in the entrance recess with her foot, as if it might be quicksand. Then she is away and I turn to face Duff again, to engage his attention and give the girl every chance to get across the playground. She's down the steps now and I can hear the skipping, diminishing rhythm of her footsteps. Got the idea now. Good girl. A nice bright kid. Soon be back with her ma.

Duff grins with a wince of the pain he showed before.

'It's as well she went, Billy,' I say. 'You're in deep enough shit without her.'

'That a fact?' he says, easing himself upright against the wall, the gun almost slipping from the tangle of his fingers. 'Well, if I'm in the shit, then I'm in the fuckin' shit. Nothin' to be done about it.'

'Could be,' I say. 'You could come out there with me. Now. It'd make things a lot easier. For everybody. You included.'

'Nah,' he says, rubbing his eyes. 'There's nothin' out there for me now.' He looks at the gun with a weak admiration, eyeing its shaft, the wooden stock, testing its weight as if with a newly acquired, precious expertise. 'They got guns?'

'No. Not that I know of,' I lie. 'Oh come on, Billy. Let's go.'

'I'm goin' nowhere.'

'What are you going to prove by staying here? You'll have to give yourself up some time.'

'Nothin'. Nothin' left to prove. Done it all. Finished now. Through with it.'

'You're not finished . . .'

'Killed somebody, 'aven't I?'

The declaration hangs solidly between us, an irreducible truth against which I can say nothing. I look across at the open door. It moves minutely in the breeze. And I'm feeling languorous, tender, perfectly drained by the excesses of the day, seduced by the extraordinary peace of the room. For all my recklessness, all the waywardness in my head, I have done well. Been lucky. I can get out of it all now with no blemish on my record, the story of my life. Duff would not stop me if I wanted to leave – the history is his now for the making: an inglorious, futile incident in which I need take no further part. I put my hands in my pockets and seat myself on the desk the girl has left. I know I cannot go.

'D'you want me to stay with you?'

'Please yourself,' he says.

So, there is silence. An hour of it. More. And from outside there is no word, no sign of movement or concern. It's almost as if they've all gone home and left us to our devices – a splendid fantasy with which I entertain myself while I'm watching Duff alternate between dozing and a wakefulness when he seems hardly aware that he is not alone. At one point he comes round with a start, looking directly at me. He begins mumbling, feverishly. I ask him if he wants to talk, but he seems incapable of deciding either yes or no. Then he is fully awake, stirring from his place by the wall, getting only as far as kneeling before he slips back again, leaning on his elbow. Thinking we might talk now, feeling conceitedly bored myself, I ask him where he got the gun. He says he bought it from old Wattsie. Bugger was out of drink. Voices driving him crazy. Sold it to Duff for half the money he'd taken from the till in the old man's shop. It was an hour after he'd killed the fellow and he was shaking like mad. Couldn't stop it. Didn't really know why he wanted a gun. Needed to defend himself, somehow. Didn't know what to expect. How could he know?

Then he's telling me about the next day, when the shaking's stopped and he just feels miserable, like he's ended up in the bottom of a deep dark well. He's been wandering the streets all night. No one's spotted him. Wouldn't have cared if they had. It's morning and he's sitting in an old truck in the railway sidings, watching a double line of police searching the yards. He's only a few hundred feet from them. They need only look up to see him. But they don't. Soft cunts. And when they've gone he simply goes into that old shed and claims it for himself. I laugh at this. We both do. Then he says he stayed there the whole damn fortnight, seeing nobody, with only the passing trains for company. He likes them, likes to hear them rumbling by, to wonder where people are going. Liked them when he was a kid. Everybody likes trains, don't they? But after a few days his head begins to bother him. He has the worst headache in the world. And he's thirsty in that old shed, hasn't eaten in all this time. So he gets water from an old metal tank in one of the yards. Tastes of metal. Gives him the shits. Fucking disgusting, that was. Then one morning he's just out, walking the streets, this big drum pounding from somewhere in his guts to the top of his head.

'Y'know,' he says after a pause. 'I never set out to kill that old bloke. Didn't plan it or nothin'.'

'I couldn't believe you did, Billy.'

'It's just that he was sort of in the way. I went into the shop an' I wanted somethin'. Didn't know what. An' 'e was just, like not goin' to give it to me. Like nobody ever gives you anything. And I got so's I couldn't stop myself. Just kept at 'im like I was fightin' the whole fuckin' world. On an' on. Didn't think to stop. Didn't know how to. An', d'you know, I can't remember hittin' anybody before in my whole life.'

'That doesn't surprise me, Bill.'

'So why'd I do it, then?'

'Don't know.'

'Don't even know what 'is fuckin' name was.'

'That'd make a difference, would it?'

'Nah,' he says, screwing his eyes tight and forcing them

[193]

open again. 'Best I don't know. Better I don't know a thing
about 'im.'

Then, from outside, from the huge waiting world beyond
the covered windows, comes King's voice, made booming and
tinny by the megaphone. '*Come on, William Duff. Time to call it
a day. Now. Don't you think? Let's see you, lad. Let's see you both.
Make your way to the window by the door. Show yourselves and
we'll take it from there. Right?*'

The intrusion makes me angry. King doesn't know Duff. Not
the way I do. He's being clumsy, fouling things up.

Duff looks up when the voice stops, as if only abortively
reminded of the circumstances.

'We'll have to let them know something,' I suggest, carefully
as I can. 'What if we both go to the window? You could stand
behind me and I'll hold my arms up.'

'Like you're 'ostage!' he says, laughing feebly. 'Gimme all
your money or the big guy gets it!'

'Right!' I say, laughing with him.

But his laughter peters away in a fit of coughing.

'Aw, I don't know. Sounds daft.'

'It was only a joke. I've got another idea,' I say, stirring myself
for the first time in two hours.

On a big side shelf, in the half-darkness of the room, I
find a child's painting of a black fierce-mouthed monster. I
turn it over to its blank side and with a thick wax crayon
lying loose on the shelf I scrawl a message. I cross the
room and slip it in front of one of the blinds. It says, 'Just
talking.'

Duff sleeps again. I find a comfortable place myself near the
front of the room, sitting on the floor with my back to the
wall. To my right, near the door, are snapshots of the children
unfathomably linked to each other with threads of wool.
Outside, the light seems to be fading prematurely. I smoke
a cigarette, then two more. The sound of a motor reaches
me from somewhere in a far reach of the playground and

the windows are suddenly illuminated by electric light, arc lamps perhaps, two of them appearing at each extremity of the building. Duff stirs again and I call to him to let him know I have moved position and that he's not to worry about the light. But he simply starts talking again as if there has been no interlude. He tells me about a dream he's had where he's in a huge warehouse, some place big enough to stage a war. He has this terrific rifle and a fantastic black uniform. Him and his little army charge the enemy across the floor of the room. He has four big men under his command and between them they take out dozens of the advancing soldiers. Then all hell breaks loose and they're away up to the roof where they escape in a flying suitcase.

His laugh is watery and he sits upright again, his head in view above the now sharp shadows of window frames and desks. He looks around himself, quite unconcerned by the new light in the room. 'Been here before,' he says, soberly.

Not so long ago. He's just happened down this part of town, late at night. He gets in through an open window of the main building, wanders the corridors, half-dreaming, looking for the kids, someone to play with. He sits down at one of the desks thinking it'll soon be break time and they'll all be out in the playground. Just him and the other kids – his mates. If it's been snowing they'll be able to make a slide, have snowball fights. And maybe they'd get into bother with the teacher. Wouldn't matter, though. They'd stick together. That's what mates do – they help each other.

Then he's telling me he's fourteen years old, standing in the street watching his mother's fancy man packing his car. Off to Spain, she says. Got to go. Tommy's business problems an' that. Be a good kid for your Auntie Bella. She'll send for him when they've got settled. He watches her go from the end of the street. He doesn't wave goodbye. Fucking good riddance, he's thinking. Better off without her. Would have been better still if he'd never known who the old cow was, like he'd never known his old man.

'Sometimes,' he says in his parched voice, 'I've like this idea where I'm in the middle of this machine. It's big, but not as big as this room. An' it sort of does anythin' I want it to. Shows me films. Feeds me an' that. Carries all the bad thoughts away, the crap. There's no way I can be sad in that thing. An' I don't 'ave to go outside for anythin' neither. Don't need money or any of that shit. Does this sound daft? Or what? S'just I've this idea of bein' where nobody can bother me . . .'

Night must be here by now. It's in my imagination – the terrible beauty of twilight dabbed away by the burgeoning darkness. Duff rolls over to his other side to sleep again. The rest will do him good. He needs the rest, needs to be whole again. But then he's never been that way, not fully made, properly born or conceived.

He's sleeping more heavily than before, his snoring inter-rupted by odd slurping noises. I doze for an hour myself, dreamless sleep scarcely beyond the veil of this dreadful reality. When I wake it's to hear movements outside, the urgent-sounding arrival of vehicles in some part of the school grounds. Soon they'll come for him, barging in, their bits of metal blazing. That horrible din. Maybe they won't kill him. Not just yet. But for the rest, the days that will follow for him in some dark dead hole . . .

I go over to him, kneeling on the floor beside his crouched body. He looks more childlike than ever. I cradle his head on my thighs. He wakes, smiles, his fingertips light about the wooden stock of the gun. And we both know what we must do. It's as if it has already happened, as if the act itself scarcely matters. He lifts the gun to his ear. But he's weak. So weak. He looks at me again. Smiles. I am to help him. It need not be said. I shuffle over him like a lover, kiss his forehead, squeeze him until he cannot breathe. Then I'm spreading my fingers over his, grasping the machinery of his little toy, easing the barrel up against his temple. He nods. Then shakes his head, a feeble resistance in his fingers. But I'm pulling both our hands tight now, about the stock, the trigger.

And the noise is nothing against my grief.

PART 4

At this time of day the town looks at ease with itself, the wet roofs of the houses glinting gold in the sunlight, the smoke from the liquorice factory a reassuring reminder of life that goes on, world without end. Early this morning I went for a walk and it was uncommonly warm, a fine dawn light in the alleys, a rare car speeding through the streets. Everything was almost shockingly familiar, so welcoming that I had the feeling that I was walking through my own mind. Then it struck me that it was also the mind of the town, that both it and I were indivisible – a single being thinking kindly of itself at last. It was a happy hour, until the streets began to thicken with people and the spell became unreliable, illusory, eventually gone.

My route home took me by a lake. It is not a beautiful place – man-made to drain a site for an industrial complex – though the reeds and hawthorns are crawling high over its white concrete corners, and birdsong competes insistently with intermittent clangs from a new car parts factory. Today, all was quiet and I walked the edge alone, slowly, as walkers there do, knowing its artificiality, perceiving something of its obscure relationship with the fabric of the town. Here one might both confront and escape oneself, sense and yet evade the weight of this society, its burden. Then, away down the banking, at the water's edge, I saw a few small children – three boys, two girls, if I remember rightly. The girls were holding bright little buckets in their hands, quietly looking to the boys who were patiently dragging fishing nets through the water. I stopped to

[201]

watch them, feeling a little light-headed every time one of them rushed a net from the depths to examine its contents, picking out bits of grass before tipping their tiny catches into one of the outheld buckets.

For a long time I waited, seeing the wind making palm prints on the lake's surface. It would have been so easy to simply slip into the water, to end it all there and then. But I knew I could not, could never, among such innocence and hope, leave the ghost of a disaffected, middle-aged man, worrying the children at their play, in their growing up. Such shame. So pointless. And I had my answer, its arrival seeming to trouble the kids, borne to them by the wind perhaps, since they suddenly threw down their gear and began scattering like footloose fawns along the banking, their sport instantly, perplexingly abandoned. Boys and girls alike, they herded into a wild threshing knot, arms lashing like white blades before they dispersed again, one of them crying, slower than the rest. Soon, though, all had disappeared.

And perhaps this conclusion of mine, made then, that I should never lift my hand against myself, somehow circulated in the consciousness I thought I had discovered this morning, made it into the air, alerted all who have known me, made them remember the social worker, that bungling player in the game of absolution. There was certainly one who was thinking about me. She was there when I rounded the corner into my street, pacing outside my door, wearing a pink patent leather coat and mint green shoes.

'Came last night,' Angela said. 'There were no answer.'

'Must have been asleep,' I said.

'Knocked bleedin' loud enough. There was a light on upstairs.'

'Probably left it on by mistake. Getting forgetful in my old age. Why did you come?'

'Just to say, yer know, sorry.'

'Oh?'

'For messin' you about an' that. I know you've 'ad a rough time of it lately. With that lad an' all.'

'History now,' I said impassively, evenly, getting used to the sound of my voice again after these last few weeks alone.

'Yeah, but you could've done without me muckin' everything up.'

'Forget it.'

'No, well, I felt proud of yer. Savin' that little girl, I mean. You got to be a hero.'

'Did I? Can't say I felt like one.'

'Must 'ave been awful, though. T'lad doin' himself in like he did. An' you just 'avin' to sit there an' watch. You know, like you said in the paper.'

I smiled, breathing out fully.

'And how are things with, you know . . .'

'Me an' Malcolm?'

'Yes.'

'S'over. Just a bit of a lark, really. Couldn't stand the stutterin' in the end. What a slobberer!'

'Hardly his fault.'

'No,' she said. 'Suppose not.' She looked down at her feet, frowning at them as if they had no right to be there, standing on the paving slabs. 'You gonna invite me in, then?'

I put my hands deep into my trouser pockets, shrugged, smiled with the same embarrassment that was affecting her.

'Best not.'

She bit at her bottom lip, shook her head, then grabbed me clumsily, kissing my cheek.

'Any time . . . you know.'

'Yes, Angela. I know. Thank you.'

And she tottered off, slowly at first, wiping something from her face, then at a brisk and businesslike pace to the end of the street and away, not caring to look round.

Soon I shall own up to my part in the Duff affair. I have suffered my guilt for too long. King, who hailed me as a hero, a saint, to all who would listen, will not believe me. Not at first, since it's true, true enough that I told him Duff had taken his own life, that I'd pleaded with him not to, that the blood on my clothes came from a desperate attempt to revive him. Before the inquest I shall point out my deception to King, confessing, yes, that I killed the boy, and suggesting that maybe we all had a hand in it, one way or another. Certainly the man will try to make me forget all about it, usher me aside, telling me to go home and take a few more days off from my demanding job. And it will be hard to prove, impossible, perhaps – I don't even know if they still have the body, though I've pictured it often enough, in some hole in the hospital mortuary wall, the big teeth smiling in the darkness, the lad's freedom, a silence of sorts, achieved at last. The gun, too, will yield no evidence, even supposing they still have it. But I'm hungry to be accountable, to insist that Duff's death was the result of my misguided altruism, my fault. And I'll have nothing to do with forgiveness, wanting no more now than to pay for my sins with my liberty, my shame, the loathing I expect to inspire. This is my decision.

And when I'm brought before the court, I trust there will be no mention of my despair. Of that I have said too much. Or maybe it was just enough?

Either way, no more.